... AND ̶ ̶ ̶ ̶ ̶ ̶ ̶ ̶ RE OF
T̶ ̶ ̶ ̶ ̶ ̶ ̶

Brian Aldiss OBE was a fiction and science fiction writer, poet, playwright, critic, memoirist and artist. Born in Norfolk in 1925, after leaving the army Aldiss worked as a bookseller which provided the setting for his first book, *The Brightfount Diaries* (1955). His first published science fiction work, the story 'Criminal Record', appeared in *Science Fantasy* in 1954. Passing away in 2017, over the course of his life Aldiss wrote nearly 100 books and over 300 short stories – becoming one of the pre-eminent science fiction writers of the 20th and 21st centuries.

Also by Brian Aldiss and published by HarperCollins

BRIAN ALDISS

AND THE LURID GLARE OF THE COMET

HARPER
Voyager

Harper*Voyager*
An imprint of HarperCollins*Publishers* Ltd
1 London Bridge Street
London SE1 9GF

www.harpercollins.co.uk

HarperCollins*Publishers*
1st Floor, Watermarque Building, Ringsend Road
Dublin 4, Ireland

First published in Great Britain in 1985 by Serconia Press

This paperback edition published by HarperCollins*Publishers* 2021
1

A catalogue record for this book is available from the British Library

ISBN: 978-0-00-748271-9

Typeset in Sabon Lt Std by Palimpsest Book Production Ltd,
Falkirk, Stirlingshire

Printed and bound in the UK by
CPI Group (UK) Ltd, Croydon CR0 4YY

Note on the text

The text of this edition was generated by scanning an earlier print copy of this collection in its first edition. The articles are presented here as they were in that publication. The writing is a product of its period and may contain themes or viewpoints now considered outdated.

Dedicated to
Gerry J. Anderson
and his friends in
Churubusco, Indiana
by
The Author of *Helliconia*

CONTENTS

Introductory Note

The idea of this book is to preserve some of the articles I have written over recent years which may be of more than ephemeral interest. It follows on from my earlier Serconia Press book, *The Pale Shadow of Science*, and is the same mixture as before. Except.

Except that here I include a brief autobiography, presenting it to my readers with some trepidation. Gale Research Books in Detroit have begun a rather astonishing series of volumes, entitled *Contemporary Authors – Autobiography Series*. Gale sent me a copy of Volume 1, asking me if I would write for Volume 2. Writers are allowed to have photographs of their choice to accompany the text. It all looks amateur and artless, but from it a reader can learn a great deal about that ever-mysterious subject, other people's lives. I decided to have a go at Volume 2.

It is difficult, perhaps impossible, to be truthful about oneself. I did my best. The exercise opened up a new area of writing. Gale limits its writers to a certain number of words. In the greatly revised sketch, here presented as 'The

Glass Forest', the thing has grown almost half as long again. My trepidation is, in consequence, almost half as great again.

Incidentally, it is worth anyone's while looking up the Gale books in their library. The first volume contains auto-biographical sketches by Marge Piercy, Richard Condon, Stanislaw Lem, and Frederik Pohl, among other familiar names, the second Poul Anderson, James Gunn, and Alan Sillitoe.

'The Glass Forest' is the *pièce de resistance* on this menu; but I hope that the other courses will also please. As before, science fiction and writing rub shoulders with travel, history, and other arts.

My thanks go as ever to the stalwarts of Serconia Press and to Marshall B. Tymn, President of the International Association for the Fantastic in the Arts, in connection with that august event, the Seventh Conference of the IAFA in Houston, Texas on March 12th–16th, 1986, which I was privileged to attend as Guest of Honour.

B.W.A.

Bold Towers, Shadowed Streets . . .

As I was finishing the compilation of this book, it happened that I received a letter from a reader in Churubusco, Indiana, Mr Gary J. Anderson. Not only was this the first time I had ever heard from any of the citizens of Churubusco, but Mr Anderson had encouraging things to say to me.

He and his friends had much enjoyed my Helliconia novels. My opinion of Churubusco went up in leaps and bounds. And in one sentence, Mr Anderson said what an author would most like to hear. He said, 'Your books have made a profound change in the way I observe things in this world.'

Your books have made a profound change in the way I observe things in this world. It's a fine sentence. I started thinking of all the books which have changed the way I observed things. When I wrote back to Mr Anderson – as I did immediately, even dropping the darling new novel on which I had just begun work – I mentioned one such book to him, *Civilisation*, by Clive Bell.

Civilisation profoundly changed the way I observed things. Let me see if I can explain the small miracle.

After over three years in the Far East, I had returned to England. 'So, you're back to civilisation at last,' said old friends. I believed the Far East to be a civilised and decent place, but I understood what they meant. Also, my role had supposedly been that of defender of civilisation. That was what you were told when you were sent to fight the Japanese, and the savage behaviour of the Japanese lent credence to the claim. And I believed the claim in the way you believe things as an adolescent, neither believing nor disbelieving, indeed hardly listening. Another thing was that at the end of the war a lot of people talked about restoring civilised values.

So I went into this used bookshop and found a book called *Civilisation* and bought it. It presented a whole new concept for consideration. Such a matter had never entered my head before. Nor had I realised what a barbarian was. Clive Bell was one of the Bloomsbury set. He married Vanessa Stephen, Virginia Woolf's sister. He was one of the elite. He would not have had a good word to say about me. I was one of his barbarians.

All the same, I liked his book greatly. Books – yes, even novels – should tell us all the things we need to know which our parents, in their ghastly struggle for a living and a false image, fail to tell us. I recognised that what Bell was saying was true (in other words, more accurately, I was swayed by his argument). For Bell, civilisation was a fragile and rather artificial structure, the chief characteristics of which were a love of music, humour, broadminded tolerance, and reason. In order to say what a revelation this was to me, I have to make the admission that until then – child of war shortages that I was – I had believed that civilisation could be defined mainly by plentiful consumer goods. In a flash, I saw how despicable was this materialist assumption. Civilisation was not a Mercedes but an attitude of mind.

This may make me sound very silly. In youth we are very silly, and things are often no better in age. The point was, I suppose, that no one had bothered to inform me of these things before, just as possibly no one had told Mr Gary Anderson that all life on Earth forms a unity.

There is another point, come to think of it. Only on certain people can such gobbets of information or revelation have effect. Stony ground abounds. I was ready for the words of Clive Bell because I had, since early childhood, been secretly aghast at the materialism of my own family. And my sojourn in the East had persuaded me that there was more than one sort of civilised behaviour.

While we are about it, I have another confession to make. Clive Bell was a great admirer of the eighteenth century. At that time, I knew rather less about the eighteenth century than I did about the moon. (About the moon I reckoned to know most of what was going, and had every faith in its being visited by mankind within the next thousand years . . .)

So I started reading about the eighteenth century, devouring some of the writings of those who lived then, studying its artists. Samuel Johnson presented himself to me, and he too changed the way I thought, rather in the way that bulls change china shops.

But I must not go on this way or I shall lose credibility. Let's stop there. Let's not make too much of *Civilisation*. It has come to seem slightly precious, *presque* Bloomsbury. But supposing Bell, who died in 1962, returned to Earth and picked up my novel, *Dark Light Years*. Would he be able to see in it some of his own teaching? I hope so.

Avid for more writings which would provide an overview of our culture, I lighted on Lewis Mumford, author of *Technics and Civilisation*. He also wrote *The Condition of Man* and *The Culture of Cities*. These I read with avidity. Like Bell, Mumford had wit, which requires a fine eye for detail.

I turn to my bookshelves to find one or other of my two copies of *Civilisation*. I have Kenneth Clarke's volume of that name, but not Clive Bell's. Somehow, they had gone, borrowed or lost in one of the Aldisses' many moves. Somehow, I had managed to live several years without wanting to look inside those covers again. Maybe the umbilical cord had been severed.

My idea had been to quote something apposite, to give a flavour of the man. Perhaps it is as well I have no copy; even good wines lose their flavour with time. Some Mumford will serve instead.

My copy of *The Culture of Cities* belonged to Arnold Toynbee, and has his signature. The book was published in 1938. Mumford is a kind of socialist-liberal or liberal-socialist much like H. G. Wells. His style, I see now, is more bombastic than my present taste enjoys. But here's what he says about metropolises, taken pretty much at random.

This metropolitan world . . . is a world where the great masses of people, unable to have direct contact with more satisfying means of living, take life vicariously, as readers, spectators, passive observers: a world where people watch shadow-heroes and heroines in order to forget their own clumsiness or coldness in love, where they behold brutal men crushing out life in a strike riot, a wrestling ring or a military assault, while they lack the nerve even to resist the petty tyranny of their immediate boss: where they hysterically cheer the flag of their political state, and in their neighbourhood, their trades union, their church, fail to perform the most elementary duties of citizenship.

Living thus, year in, year out, at second hand, remote from the nature that is outside them, and no less remote from the nature within, handicapped as lovers and as parents by the routine of the metropolis and by the constant specter of insecurity and death that hovers over its bold towers and shadowed streets – living thus the mass of inhabitants remain in a state bordering on the pathological.

And so on. To be honest, I am less carried away by such arguments than I was when I went into my Mumford phase at the end of World War II. I found myself trapped in an English city – admittedly the pleasantest of cities, Oxford – and this American voice was a comforter, not a rabble-rouser. For my time in the East had been spent mainly outdoors. The Army is not a domestic institution. The sun, the wind, the rain, were immoderate elements. None of your English compromises, when it is hard to tell whether or not the sun is up. Protestantism would never have taken root in India. There, they must have gods with fifty arms, to match the manic dexterity of nature.

Somehow, I had to fit myself into the hole of urban living, and it went hard. Mumford gave voice, with a Shakespearean command of detail, to my discontents. The city as civilisation's lens and destroyer! This was what Shelley was talking about when he wrote to his friend Maria Gisborne:

7

You are now
In London, that great sea, whose ebb and flow
At once is deaf and loud, and on the shore
Vomits its wrecks, and still howls for more.

Success is a city much like London. It too can welcome us in, only to destroy us. But is it better to fail in the countryside?

The answer to that question seems to be that those who amass fortunes, and who are therefore most able to choose, prefer, on the whole, the vivid physical life of the hunt, whether the quarry be fish, fox, or fallow deer, at a good distance from the nearest metropolis.

In those bold towers and shadowed streets of which Mumford speaks, decisions are being taken which will influence all of us. We cannot expect with any confidence that those decisions will have our good at heart. We are surrounded with plenty, with a hailstorm of technological marvels, with a variety of foods and drinks such as the ancient pharaohs never knew, with immense personal freedoms (freedom from slavery, for instance – a rare thing in the history of civilisation), with access to lakes and oceans of knowledge, with ceaseless imagery, and with the abounding creativity of our century. And yet . . . and yet the shadow of physical and spiritual famine stalks us. The lurid glare of the comet reveals the poverty of our 'dark, compressed lives,' to borrow Wells's phrase.

This is the great dilemma. Somehow, we have to control ourselves. Clive Bell, a member of the elite, believed in rule by elite. So did Plato in his *Republic*, and More after him, in *Utopia*, and most of the utopianists since. In my novel, *The Malacia Tapestry*, I tried to draw a city state utopia ruled by an elite. Malacia is a sunny, not unhappy place, but eventually the sheer human injustice of it becomes intolerable, even to those – like my hero, de Chirolo – who don't wish to think about such matters.

We have to believe in the equality of mankind, even though our daily experience tells us that equality does not exist. At least equality can exist in the mind.

Equality implies self-discipline. If my neighbour is my equal, I shall not mug him. If I am the equal of my neighbour, again, I shall not mug him. If those shadowy decision-makers in the bold towers think we are all equal, they will not metaphysically mug us.

Well, I can see that these are topics I ought to confine within the perimeters and ill-defined shores of my new and yet unwritten novel. As a popular writer, I believe in the success of the popular arts, and in the duty of those arts to demonstrate that there is more to life than a succession of Rambos and Conans. No one can be equal in the lands of Rambo and Conan. There is a better world, where complex issues are decided by other than blows and bullets.

May it long continue so, in Oxford and Churubusco!

... And the Lurid Glare of the Comet

'Others abide our question – thou art free,' said Matthew Arnold in his sonnet on Shakespeare. Among past science fiction writers, many, I fear, abide our question and are gone. Wells, on the other hand, seems in many respects to increase in stature. He is our Shakespeare.

We know little of William Shakespeare outside his writings. Of H. G. Wells, we are well informed. His is a tightly documented life. Not only are his fictions grounded in his own life, however finely above ground they fly; he took care to leave various records of what he was up to. He lived at a brisk pace and did not easily separate life from literature. This trait it was that lured him into much of the hasty journalism with which he became involved, and which has obscured his real achievements.

Bernard Bergonzi's seminal work, *The Early H. G. Wells*, has established a kind of orthodoxy: that the early science fiction is the best of Wells, and that little he wrote after *The First Men in the Moon* in 1901 is of much consequence. This is not entirely true, or is at best a simplification. There is the almost unconsidered *In the Days of the Comet*, for instance.

Of recent years, we have had to adjust our views of Herbert George Wells. It was becoming easy for a general reader simply to dismiss him as a failed prophet, or to classify him with such writers of a fading epoch as Arnold Bennett, Gissing, or Hilaire Belloc. But Wells is amazing; Wells had a time-bomb waiting. In 1984 was published – thirty-eight years after his death – his secret story of his love-lives, under the title *H. G. Wells in Love*.

Wells wanted to be happy, that most immodest of ambitions. He took great pains to be happy, and devoted much of his remarkable energy to that end; what was rare in his strivings was that he tried to make the women with whom he so regularly got himself involved happy too. He set them up in houses, paid their hotel bills, and for many years put up with the most difficult of them (there the palm goes to Odette Keun) in a vague placatory way which must have aggravated as much as it mollified. The most famous of these involvements, apart from that with his breathtakingly tolerant second wife, Jane, was with Rebecca West.

There was, of course, Rebecca West's side of the question; but our later age can see sympathetically that many of the vexing contrivances these lovers were put to, as for instance the occasional pretence that Wells was merely his son Anthony's uncle, were forced upon them by the social conventions of the time.

This great amorous warfare of flesh and spirit comes fresh to mind as one reads *In the Days of the Comet*. The book was first published in 1906, at a time Wells labelled 'the promiscuous phase of my life'; not that he was able exactly to stay chaste until well into his seventies. By 1906 Wells was extremely famous in a way that writers these days are not, who sink instead into obscurity, produce plays, or become 'media personalities'. Wells went travelling about the world, enjoying intercourse of one kind or another with presidents and prostitutes, reporting and being reported on. He was confident that a new world was emerging, uncertain how it would emerge, eternally lively and curious. A natural advocate of free love.

Once his book of essays, *Anticipations*, had been published in 1901, Wells was listened to increasingly as a prophetic voice, competent to speak about the real world, rather than to indulge merely in his ingenious fantasies. *In the Days of the Comet* is a balance between the dissatisfactions and hope of the real world and constructive fantasy. It's a visionary novel. Visionary novels are always disappointing in some way, since words never correspond exactly to either facts or wishes; but this is a prize exhibit of the species.

Wells's first readers were most struck by his vision of the new world emerging, a world of free love and social equality. We in our generation are more likely to be impressed by his portrait of things as they were – and by their resemblance to today. The comet has yet to come.

A profile of the novel appears disarmingly simple, a case of 'Look here upon this picture, and on this.' We are shown the old world; the comet passes; we are shown the new world. There is a Biblical directness in the parable: 'We shall all be changed, in a moment, in the twinkling of an eye.' The comet is the mechanism, the lurid visitant, which carries us from the one picture to the other, and Wells is properly offhand in his pseudo-scientific talk of the nitrogen in the comet's tail having its benevolent effects upon mankind.

This sensible method of argument by contrast is one that others have followed, before and since. We hope for a better world, we see it clear. But how to get there? Wells in 1906 could see no bridge to utopia; he forged a miracle instead, with legitimate didactic intent.

This forging is performed with great literary skill – something with which Wells is too little credited (though Nabokov and Eliot have acknowledged Wells's powers). The strengths of the book have also been widely underestimated, even by those writers and readers who traffic in comets and similar wonders.

The story is told in Wells's easy manner. After a crisis, we get the throwaway remark, 'Then, you know, I suppose I folded up this newspaper and put it in my pocket,' which catches without pretention the absent-minded listlessness following a lover's quarrel. The prose grows more spirited when Wells's traditional dislikes are paraded. Despite many attempts at it since, no one has bettered Wells's description of places where commerce has invaded nature – perhaps because he finds a kind of desolate beauty there. When Leadford, the central character, arrives at a seaside town, we come on the following passage:

The individualistic enterprise of that time had led to the plotting out of nearly all the country round the seaside towns into roads and building plots – all but a small portion of the south and east coast was in this condition, and had the promises of those schemes been realised the entire population of the island might have been accommodated upon the sea frontiers. Nothing of the sort happened, of course; the whole of this uglification of the coastline was done to stimulate a little foolish gambling in plots, and one saw everywhere agents' boards in every state of freshness and decay, ill-made exploitation roads overgrown with grass, and here and there at a corner, a label, 'Trafalgar Avenue' or 'Sea View Road'. Here and there, too, some small investor, some shopman with 'savings' had delivered his soul to the local builders and built himself a house; and there it stood, ill-designed, mean-looking, isolated, ill-placed on a cheaply fenced plot, athwart which his domestic washing fluttered in the breeze amidst a bleak desolation of enterprise.

Of course we recognize it. What was happening in Shaphambury in 1906 is happening in Florida today.

The tale of Leadford's thwarted affair with Nellie, of his love which turns to hatred, and of the business with the gun, is occasionally melodramatic; a similar theme is more subtly handled in the 1924 novel, *The Dream*. But the narrative proves enough to allow Wells to string out before us a series of ghastly cameos, the finest of which is probably the picture of the industrial Midlands, when twilight settled over a tawdry scene of sheds, factories, terrace houses, and blast furnaces.

Each upstart furnace, when its monarch sun had gone, crowned itself with flames, the dark cinder heaps began to glow with quivering fires, and each pot-bank squatted rebellious in a volcanic coronet of light. The empire of the day broke into a thousand feudal baronies of burning coal.

14

Such passages brim with imaginative energy. In his book, *Language of Fiction*, David Lodge makes an eloquent defence of *Tono-Bungay*, which Wells was to publish only three years after *In the Days of the Comet*. Lodge points out that there is a way of reading Wells, just as there is of reading Henry James, and speaks of *Tono-Bungay* as a 'Condition of England' novel: a novel neglected because its style, its whole thrust, does not accord with preconceived ideas of the English novel as formulated by Henry James and F. R. Leavis. To a large extent, the same principle applies to *In the Days of the Comet*.

All its vivid imagery of physical chaos serves a purpose directly geared to the meaning of the novel. It links the tangible world with the chaos of mankind's thinking, and in particular with Leadford's lost and murderous state of mind. As we are told,

The world of thought in those days was in the strangest condition, it was choked with obsolete inadequate formulae, it was tortuous to a maze-like degree with secondary contrivances and adaptations, suppressions, conventions, and subterfuges. Base immediacies fouled the truth on every man's lips.

Clarity was blocked as thoroughly as the way to the sea.

In fact, Wells offers his readers a red herring in the extract quoted above. 'The world of thought' may indeed have been choked by 'contrivances, adaptations, suppressions, conventions, and subterfuges'; but this emotive description applies even more closely to Wells's private 'world of emotions,' to what he termed 'the promiscuous phase of his life'. The utopia of the novel is no extensive plan of rational living,

as were previous utopias such as Bellamy's, whose rationale
Wells had borrowed for *When the Sleeper Wakes*, or even
as were Wells's earlier approaches towards utopia. Rather,
it is a sphere where love requires no 'contrivances', etc.

Linking *In the Days of the Comet* with *The Dream*,
Patrick Parrinder, in an article on Wells's utopias, says that
the novel stresses 'not the perfection of social organisation
in a utopia but the contrast between the individual content-
ment it would offer and the emotional storm and stress of
twentieth century life.'*

For ten years, Wells had poured out his mythopoeic stories
and novels in extravagant, generous, and startling fashion.
Really, a decade of such prodigality is all we should expect
from any writer: burning out is also part of the giving process
of creativity. There is textual reason to believe that Wells,
that intuitive creature, was aware of the passing of his gift.
In the same year that *In the Days of the Comet* appeared,
one of Wells's best short stories was published in a daily
newspaper; its theme runs parallel to the theme of the novel.

In 'The Door in the Wall', Lionel Wallace, the central
figure, grows up to be a successful public figure. At the age
of five, he is wandering the city streets near home when he
discovers the door in the wall. He enters, to find himself in
a garden of delight, the original primal garden, where
panthers are harmless and gentle mother figures attend him.
There are other children in the garden. They greet Lionel
with friendly cries. He plays with them. The garden is a
personal utopia for one.

Once he has left the garden, Lionel can never find it again.

* Patrick Parrinder, 'Utopia and Meta-Utopia in H. G. Wells'; *SF Studies*
  36, July 1985.

16

He grows up. He becomes a member of parliament, a Cabinet Minister. Occasionally, after long intervals, he sees the door again, but can never spare time to enter it. Always some worldly business prevents him: he is hurrying to see a woman or he is late getting to the House of Commons. His sense of lost vision grows as he grows older.

> This loss is destroying me. For two months, for ten weeks nearly now, I have done no work at all, except the most necessary and urgent duties. My soul is full of unappeasable regrets . . . .

Wells celebrated his fortieth birthday in 1906. 'The Door in the Wall', like *In the Days of the Comet*, shows a weariness with the humdrum world, a longing for illumination, a hatred for the smallness of everyday life. Yet Wells was fated to enter that life, to become a businessman of ideas, now that his creative fire was dying. Bergonzi puts it differently: 'His imagination became increasingly coerced by his intellectual convictions.'

It may be so. What is less arguable is Bergonzi's perception that the door in the wall, which remained forever closed and eventually resulted in the death of Lionel, stands as a symbol of the highly original talent which Wells sensed he was losing.

The experienced writer has his strategies. Most of Wells's writing life still lay before him. He found a way to eke out the imaginative with various intellectual speculations which were interesting in themselves. And he found subjects nearer home than Mars and the Moon. In particular, he found England and the twentieth century.

* * *

Consider two brief passages from *In the Days of the Comet*, in which we are asked respectively to perceive the inner and outer lives of men of the twentieth century, and of the central character in particular.

> We young people had practically no preparation at all for the stir and emotions of adolescence. Toward the young the world maintained a conspiracy of stimulating silences. There came no initiation. There were books, stories of a curiously conventional kind that insisted on certain qualities in every love-affair and greatly intensified one's natural desire for them, perfect trust, perfect loyalty, lifelong devotion. Much of the complex essentials of love were altogether hidden .... We were like misguided travellers who had camped in the dry bed of a tropical river. Presently we were knee deep and neck deep in the flood.

And:

> To the left spread a darkling marsh of homes, an infinitude of little smoking hovels, meagre churches, public houses, Board schools, and other buildings out of which the prevailing chimneys of Swathinglea rose detachedly. To the right, very clear and relatively high, the Bantock Burden pit-mouth was marked by a gaunt lattice bearing a great black wheel, sharp and distinct in the twilight, and beyond, in an irregular perspective, were others following the lie of the seams. The general effect, as one came down the hill, was of a dark compressed life beneath a very high and wide and luminous evening sky, against which those pit-wheels rose. And ruling the calm spaciousness of that

heaven was the great comet, now green-white, and wonderful for all who had eyes to see.

Over the chaos shines the comet, growing larger night by night. It forms a contrast to the 'dark, compressed life' on which it shines. Wells wrote with the predicted 1910 appearance of Halley's comet in mind. Equally topical for us is the miner's strike, with its pickets and attacks on cars. Wells's power as a fantasist derives from his firm grip of the world-as-it-is.

Since *In the Days of the Comet* was not well received when it appeared, as frequently happens when visionary books are set before a largely unprepared public, it seems appropriate to offer a new reading of the novel to a new set of readers.

This is not a 'Condition of England' novel, though in some respects it may be seen as a precursor of *Tono-Bungay*. Rather, it is a skilfully conducted 'Condition of Mind' novel. The Change effected by the comet is a change of mind. Striking descriptions of physical states are always linked to mental states – as when the hideous towns are designated 'cities men weep to enter'. The sick state of the people before the Change is dramatised cunningly in a variety of ways as Europe drifts towards war, the ultimate waste, the ultimate confusion. 'Humanity choked amidst its products.'

This sickness of mind is nowhere better embodied than in the character of its central figure, Willie Leadford, who tells the story. On the first page of his narrative, Leadford speaks of his 'crude, unhappy youth'. Throughout the story until the Change, he reveals himself as brutal, troubled, murderous, and ineffective. This is precisely the state of the world in which he lives. Despite the tide of bottled emotions, everything is reduced to pettiness. 'It seems to me even now,' says Leadford after the Change, 'that the little dark creature who had stormed across England in pursuit of Nettie and her lover must have been about an inch high . . .'

Leadford is deliberately not elaborately characterised. The same applies to the few other actors – a point to which we return later. But on the details encumbering Leadford's physical existence Wells is sharply precise. We particularly understand the nature of this 'dark and sullen lout', as he calls himself, by his treatment of his mother, the woman who endured much to ensure her son's comfort, minimal though that comfort is.

The portrait of Mrs Leadford is undoubtedly based on Wells's memory of his mother at Atlas House in Bromley, Kent, where he was born. The exasperated love he felt for her is always present, nowhere more so than in the description of the old woman's dreadful kitchen. Even George Orwell never bettered that kitchen of Mrs Leadford's, where the business of deforming the human soul is carried on quite as efficiently as in any factory. Mrs Leadford is growing old in her foul kitchen. Her hands are distorted by ill-use. She coughs. She shuffles about in badly fitting boots. Even her son wants nothing to do with her.

Wells turns to the historic present for the climax of these scenes of domestic misery. Leadford, betrayer and betrayed, says, 'And while she washes up I go out, to sell my overcoat and watch in order that I may desert her.'

In the Days of the Comet is full of such compelling moments, which crystallise the whole point of the book while being sufficiently powerful in themselves as moments of tragi-comedy in Wells's best manner.

So the entire first part of the novel represents an acute

and brilliantly drawn picture of the mind of England and the industrialised countries at the turn of the century. Leadford, taken up with his wretched emotional relationships and his socialism, pays little attention to the comet drawing nearer to Earth. His counterweight, Parload, is the astronomer; it is through Parload that we see the contrast between earthly squalor and heavenly beauty, while Leadford is still having trouble with his boots.

The comet arrives and brings the Change. Wells now draws the utopia that could be. He was always a master of symbols, in his swift, careless-seeming way. Among the first objects the changed Leadford sees are a discarded box of pills and a wrecked battleship, a 'torn and battered mass of machinery' now lying amid ploughed-up mountains of chalk ooze. From now on, it will be possible to make love, not war.

Despite all these excellent preparations, the utopian world of might-be is a shadowy place when we come to it. Wells has to resort ultimately to traditional stereotype, of a place with trees of golden fruit and crystal fountains, tenanted by people who look exalted. He confronts a difficulty that Dante and Milton faced before him; the *Inferno* and *Paradise Lost* have more readers than a thousand *Paradiso*s and *Paradise Regained*s. Not only is a better world hard to realize, even on paper; but Wells had addressed himself particularly to that subject in the previous year, with the publication of *A Modern Utopia*, and his real interest lay elsewhere.

A Modern Utopia is a full-fleshed blueprint for a better, healthier, and happier world, in which a regulated capitalist economy is presided over by an elite (the 'samurai'). Since it appeared in 1905, *A Modern Utopia* has been much sneered at. Many of the book's ideas are sensible and rational

– in a word, Wellsian; but an irrational streak in us prevents our putting our knowledge into practice on any effective scale. Wells was essentially rather a simple person (an adjective he applies affectionately to Kipps), and it was this simplicity which gave him the confidence to put forward his less-than-simple plans for mankind, generally in the expectation that they would be immediately taken up.

The rather shadowy utopia to which we are introduced at the end of the present book contains two well-dramatised elements not markedly present in *A Modern Utopia*, the death of warfare and an outspoken argument for free love. The argument for free love is carried on into the 'frame' of the story for extra emphasis.

Critics have accused Wells of wanting war. Certainly he was obsessed with war, almost as greatly as we are in our time. Certainly in 1914 he applauded the call to arms, as many people did – and wrote a rather silly book whose title coined a cliché, *The War that will End War*. But nobody reading *In the Days of the Comet* would call him a warmonger. I am thinking particularly of the lovely moment after the Change when the common soldiery on its way to war – as it might be, in Flanders – returns to consciousness by the roadside.

The men do not fall into ranks. They discuss the causes of war with incredulity. 'The Emperor!' they exclaim. 'Oh, nonsense! We're civilised men . . . . Where's the coffee?'

It did not work out that way in 1914. Halley's comet passed without effect.

But the new thing in Leadford's utopia which caught the attention in 1906 was emotional freedom. Love, not war, to suit that 'promiscuous phase' of his life.

Wells advocates free love: cleverly, he has a woman put

forward the argument. Nellie is changed from a rural face-
less creature to a 'young woman of advanced appearance'
(to borrow a description jokingly applied to Christina
Alberta in Wells's later novel *Christina Alberta's Father*). She
puts forward the argument tentatively at first, but in the
end conclusively: marriage is not what she wants; she wants
to love where she chooses; she wants both Leadford and
his rival. 'Am I not a mind that you must think of me as
nothing but a woman?'

What infuriated the righteous, and Wells's enemies in the
Fabian Society, was that Wells not only advocated free love,
but had the cheek to practise it. He defied the conventions
of the time. There is an amusing example of this in *H. G.
Wells in Love*. Before the First World War, Wells was enjoying
an affair with the Gräfin von Arnim, the Irish lady whose
book, *Elizabeth and her German Garden*, was beloved in
stately and less stately homes up and down the land.

One day Wells and von Arnim found something in the
correspondence columns of *The Times* which amused them.
It was, says Wells,

> a letter from Mrs Humphrey Ward denouncing the moral
> tone of the younger generation, apropos of a rising young
> writer, Rebecca West, and, having read it aloud, we decided
> we had to do something about it. So we stripped ourselves
> under the trees as though there was no one in the world
> but ourselves and made love all over Mrs Humphrey
> Ward. And when we had dressed again we lit a match
> and burnt her.

A word should be said finally about the form of *In the
Days of the Comet*. Although it has been referred to here

and elsewhere as a novel, it is in fact a separate if allied form, a novella. A novella, as properly understood, restricts itself to a single situation or event. It has few characters, and they mainly function in a symbolic role: the protagonist, the woman as love object, the rival, the mother, the statesman, and so on. Goethe's *Elective Affinities* is a good example of a novella. And *In the Days of the Comet* is a rare English language example of the mode – a much more perfect example than has hitherto been recognized.

In it, H. G. Wells shows his characteristic dissatisfaction with the existing order, his spirited hatred of the mess we have got ourselves into, his striving for better things. No doubt if he were alive today he would still find ample reason for dissatisfaction, hatred, striving, and contrivances.

When the Future Had to Stop

Some science fiction novels stay in the repertory too long. Others, for no good reason, never establish themselves. Or they may fail to establish themselves for a bad reason, because the author does not produce enough to keep his name perennially before the audience.

The name of Kingsley Amis is well enough known as a novelist. It is also fragrant to the sf audience as that of the author of the first general survey of sf – and an acute one at that – *New Maps of Hell*. There is also a short story or two, one an amusing parody of Ernest Hemingway, and the alternative world novel, *The Alteration*. But *Russian Hide-and-Seek* (1980) has failed to find an established place in the hearts of readers.

Perhaps it is because *Russian Hide-and-Seek* is both a rather forbidding novel and a rather complex one. This is a plea for better attention to it.

In a sense, the central topic of the novel is straight-forward, even time-honoured. Britain, owing to its lack of vigilance, has been taken over by the Russians, and is now a satellite of the Soviet Union. This seems to place the book in the dire warning category of *The Battle of Dorking* and *When the Kissing Had to Stop*.

But matters are less simple than that. It is part of Amis's cunning that he does not show us the invasion of the island. Like an Ibsen play, a lot of history has flowed under the bridge before the curtain goes up. We are confronted with a Britain fifty years after the coup.

The opening is magisterial. A grand English country house is surrounded by pastureage. The son, Alexander, an ensign in the Guards, is vexing his family, and indeed everyone else. The mother worries about flowers and dinner arrangements. We might be embarking on a leisurely nineteenth century novel. The one blemish to the rural picture seems to be the hundreds of tree stumps which disfigure the grounds of the mansion. That, and the family name, Petrovsky.

What we at first may assume to be threatened is in fact absolutely overwhelmed. There is no way to undo fifty years of history. This is an England no longer England. It is now the EDR, Soviet-occupied.

There is nothing futuristic about the EDR. It has been reduced to an imitation of pre-revolutionary Russia. This is a world of stately country homes with a vengeance, with the English as servants. Parties are thrown, dances are held, and dashing young fellers ride about on horseback. This reversion follows the somewhat similar patterns the victorious Nazis impose on Europe in Sarban's *The Sound of His Horn*, which once appeared in an edition with an admiring introduction by Kingsley Amis.

The novel is one of fine surfaces and corrupt interiors. Here is another large house. White-coated servants move about, supplying drink and food. Tennis is in progress on two courts. A small orchestra is playing old-fashioned waltzes. Everything is supposedly done in high style.

But: 'No one thought, no one saw that the clothes of the guests were badly cut from poor materials . . . that the women's coiffures were messy and the men's fingernails dirty, that the surfaces of the courts were uneven and inadequately raked, that the servants' white coats were not very white, that the glasses and plates they carried had not been properly washed, or that the pavement where the couples danced needed sweeping . . . No one thought any of that because no one had ever known any different.'

Ignoring the fact that this is rather obtrusive authorial comment, we see embodied here the fine surface / corrupt interior principle on which the novel hinges. To every thing there is another aspect.

Alexander Petrovsky starts like a hero out of Fielding, young and spirited. He makes a fine initial impression on readers – and on Commissioner Mets, the power in the land. He impresses Mets by addressing him in good English, the language of the conquered. Alexander has gone to some pains to learn a few useful phrases and to pronounce them properly. 'But his vocabulary had remained small and his ability to carry on a conversation smaller still.'

Alexander bullies his subordinates. His sexual appetites are gross, and scarcely satisfied when he encounters Mrs Korotchenko, who likes being trampled on before the sexual act, and introduces her twelve year old daughter Dasha to join in her lusty variety of fun. They perform in a kind of sexual gymnasium.

If the occupying force is shown as corrupt under its polished veneer, the English are no better. The good ones were killed off in the invasion and the Pacification. Those left are mainly

27

a pack of docile tipplers, devoid of morale and culture, living in a kind of rustic sub-world. It is a dystopia quite as convincing and discomfiting as Orwell's urban warrens.

To parallel this total loss of English qualities, the occupying force have lost all belief in their motivating creed, Marxism, which died out about 2020.

Among the younger Russian set, men and women, English phrases are fashionable. '*Fucking hell*,' says Elizabeth. The younger set imagines it is fond of England. Certain of them, including Theodore, the fiancé of Alexander's sister, are plotting to take advantage of a Moscow-generated New Cultural Policy. 'Group 31', to which Theodore belongs, plans to restore England to the English.

'Group 31' wish to get Alexander involved. He is willing enough. To be a revolutionary is a great romantic pose which panders to his narcissism. He is callously prepared to assassinate his liberal father, if need be. And of course he will get a vital list off Mrs Korotchenko, who is the wife of the Deputy Director of Security, under Director Vanag.

Unexpected deaths follow, yet the underground theme proves less exciting than it should. What is more interesting, perhaps because more unusual, is the attempt, prompted by Moscow, to launch a performance of a once banned Shakespeare play, *Romeo and Juliet*. The play is to be the climax of a festival in which English culture is handed back to the English.

The Russians do not and cannot care for the past they have obliterated. Nor do the English care – except for a few over-fifties, who scarcely count. It is true that they refer to their conquerors as *the Shits*, but this is a fossil appellation, almost without malice. By such small authentic notes, the originality of the novel declares itself.

An audience is somehow raked up to attend the great event. The music recital is moderately successful. It includes works by 'Dowland, Purcell, Sullivan, Elgar, the composer of "Ta-ra-ra-boom-de-ay," Noel Coward, Duke Ellington (taken to have been an English nobleman of some sort), Britten and John Lennon.' But with *Romeo and Juliet*, it is different.

Alexander has a drink at the Marshal Stalin in St John's Street before attending the theatre. The play about the death of innocence – although it has been cut to an hour in order not to tax people's patience too greatly – is a disaster. There is a near riot, the theatre is set on fire, Alexander decides not to rescue the girl playing Juliet.

In scenes of ghastly comedy, Shakespeare's island race rejects its old culture and religion when they are offered. It prefers to queue quietly for food – a typical meal being cabbage soup, belly of pork with boiled beets (since there's now a third fresh-meat day in a week), and stewed windfalls. Or it will booze at the Marshal Grechko (to become The Jolly Englishman under the New Cultural Policy).

Once a culture ceases to be common coinage, it has gone forever. It is a grim warning, one which elevates the novel far above the jingoistic military warning, Be Prepared! Sadness rather than jingoism is the imprint of these pages.

'Group 31' itself turns out to be a veneer over something nastier. And the insatiable Mrs Korotchenko betrays Alexander. Nor is this the only betrayal. One of the most chilling moments comes at the end, when Director Vanag is interrogating Theodore, after the latter's coup has failed. Vanag relates something of the history of the so-called Pacification, fifty years earlier. 'It was our country's chance to take what she had always wanted most, more than

Germany, far more than the Balkans, more even than America. And she took it, after serious difficulty at first, after being on the point of having to withdraw entirely in order to regroup.'

Theodore asks, 'What did the Americans do?'

Vanag begins to laugh. He never bothers to answer the question.

Fittingly, the usual Amis humour is, in *Russian Hide-and-Seek*, suffused into a permeating irony. Detail is piled on disconcerting detail – each unexpected but just – like the young English woman girlishly longing to get to Moscow (an echo of Chekhov here), until the whole disastrous tapestry of a lost England hangs before us.

All that we value has been swept away. Culture is irrelevant. Nihilism prevails.

I have to declare an interest of a special nature in *Russian Hide-and-Seek*. The novel is dedicated to my wife Margaret and me. It's a fine novel, and I'm grateful.

What Happens Next?

This piece was composed for special circumstances, which I had better explain.

My last school, referred to elsewhere in this volume, was West Buckland, in North Devon. Although I was glad to leave, one of the masters there kept in touch with me, my old housemaster, Harold Boyer. We corresponded sporadically, even when I was in the Far East.

While I was meeting with a measure of literary success, Harold became a government Inspector of Schools, and, later, a Governor of West Buckland. The school by this time had acquired a forward-looking headmaster, Michael Downward.

I always sent copies of my books to the school library, hoping they might enliven the hours of some of those incarcerated there, as the writings of Aldous Huxley, Evelyn Waugh, and H.G. Wells had enlivened my period at school. There was also a certain ironic pleasure to be had in knowing that science fiction was cordially enshrined in the establishment where, in my time, it had been forbidden. Had not our Maths master, 'Chicken' Coupland (a wartime conscientious objector) torn up a valued issue of *Astounding Science Fiction* before the eyes of the whole form, at a time when I was in the middle of reading Theodore Sturgeon's 'Biddiver'?

As if to mark how greatly things had changed, one room in the school library was now officially designated 'The Aldiss Room'. I was invited to open it.

Driving down to Devon, I took with me a carton of presentation copies and the best reproductions I could find of two paintings to hang in the room which might have some appeal to the boys there. Both paintings held an exciting essence for me, and had helped towards a cohesive imagery in my writing. The hope was that someone else would glance at them occasionally and find imaginative escape from the routines of school.

This is the talk I gave about those paintings at the opening of The Aldiss Room.

The grave, marvellous beauty of Pieter Breugel's *Hunters in the Snow* speaks for itself. If you find a prevailing sadness in it, that is in part because all the characters in the painting – and there are over fifty of them – are turned away from us, otherwise engaged. They have no concern with the external viewer, being entirely involved with their own world, their own pursuits. They remain inaccessible to us.

Hunters in the Snow is one of a series of canvasses Bruegel executed on the great secular topic of the months or seasons. Some of the series still exist after four centuries, some of them are lost. The original measures 114cm. by 158cm. – that is about 44 inches by 61 – and hangs in the Kunsthistorisches Museum in Vienna. Its power combines with apparent simplicity like a moral force.

We know little about Bruegel, but we do know that he painted this picture in 1565. Shakespeare had been born the year before. Those luminaries of the Renaissance, Veronese and Tintoretto, Bruegel's contemporaries, were working in the grand style in Italy; Palladio was building the church of St Giorgio Maggiore in Venice. As you see, Bruegel did not paint at all like the Italians. His preoccupations were different and, for my taste, more profound.

This was the period when the Spanish were making a great noise round the world. It was the age of Sir Francis Drake, when Protestants and Catholics were engaged in bitter combat, when Mary Queen of Scots married Lord Darnley, and the Duke of Alva with 10,000 troops was all set to tyrannise the Low Countries. The plague raged. And plague, war, tyranny, the beastliness of man, all find forceful expression in Bruegel's paintings.

Not in this one. This painting reminds us of the other side of that cruel period. It reminds us that renaissance means re-birth, that the world was opening out, and that, as one critic put it, a sort of 'reclassification of the universe' was taking place. It is easier to see in Bruegel than in his Italian contemporaries the birth of our own age, with his concern not for princes or religion but with common people and common pursuits.

The very shape, the stances, of his people, make them our kin. Veronese's people are classical, patrician, Bruegel's are peasants. Veronese may show us languid men, never tired ones. He has a message to proclaim; Bruegel has a new awareness.

If you visited Mao's China, you saw art bent to the common end of glorifying the state, just as one sees the art of the Italian Renaissance directed to glorifying the worldly shows of religion. Bruegel had nothing to do with all that. His paintings show him to be a sceptical man, for whom 'glory' was a relative affair.

One's response to art operates on several levels. There's the academic level – and to derive full appreciation from a work of art requires training – and the personal level. For me, the point at which Bruegel and I meet is where he demonstrates exuberantly that an organic relationship exists between humanity and nature, that mankind has his due place in the affairs of the biosphere, and that whatever he does he is wedded to the seasons and the sweep of the sun –

> Rolled round in earth's diurnal course,
> With rocks, and stones, and trees.

Against the might of the universe, man's shows count for little (it is there that Bruegel parts company with the grand Italians). In his paintings, he expresses such commonplace but profound matters in many ways. In two of his more religious paintings, *The Conversion of St Paul* and *The Procession to Calvary*, the events described in the titles – St Paul's conversion and Christ's procession with the Cross – take place. Both St Paul and Christ are placed in the traditional centre of their respective canvasses; but the crowds swarming about them, the landscapes and mountains which rise on every side, eclipse the main event. Most of the people depicted are scarcely concerned with St Paul and Christ – they have their own lives to live. This profound and novel psychological observation, this populist view of history, must have shocked the first viewers of those canvasses to an extent that we, in a less religious age, can hardly appreciate. Perhaps the humanist in Bruegel found men more interesting than gods.

There's a similar effect in one of Bruegel's most famous paintings, *The Fall of Icarus*. The mythical flier plunges down into the water. All we see of him are legs, framed in spray. The legs are a mere detail lost in the large canvas. All about lies a golden imperishable landscape, constructed in the manner of *Hunters in the Snow*, with sea in the distance and ships upon it; close at hand, on the left, a peasant follows the plough, oblivious to Icarus' tragic drama of ambition. Sailors, fishermen, a shepherd, also carry on work as usual, ignorant or innocent of the mythological event which flashes in their midst.

W.H. Auden is thinking of such a synthesis when he claims that the old masters were never wrong about suffering. Dreadful dramas were enacted on the canvas. Meanwhile,

the dogs go on with their doggy life and the torturer's horse Scratches its innocent behind on a tree.

The ploughman must be important, for he is in the foreground. Like so many of Bruegel's figures, he is generalised, not particularised. He stands for all ploughmen. But Icarus, the visionary, also has his place: it is for him the canvas is titled, just as the other canvasses are titled for St Paul and Christ. The earth's work may rest on the shoulders of the peasants but they are rarely individual, being sunk in the subculture of labour. We also need the individual, the artist, the sufferer, the thinker, who flashes across the scene, who is – unlike the peasant – remembered when gone.

Studying *Hunters in the Snow* more closely, we can

observe some of the emblems which were never far from Bruegel's thinking. The first men on our planet were hunters, and these Flemish hunters are scarcely better equipped for the hunt than were Neolithic men. They're passing a primitive inn, its sign awry, where the occupants are evidently concerned only in a very basic existence, the life of food and drink. They're roasting a pig.

The hunters are in transition. They're descending into the valley, where life is more civilised. It's a medieval world down there, still dominated by the mill which for centuries represented the latest technology and permitted an increase in the population. On the frozen stream and fields, children play, skating or sliding, permitting a glimpse of that ceaseless activity of the poor which so interested Bruegel. You may be reminded of the modern painter, L.S. Lowry, but Lowry's urban crowds are always isolated and hold no communion with each other. The hurlyburly of Bruegel's crowds is different, jollier, far more earthy.

Life looks quite tolerable. But the slow plod of the hunters, their poor catch, their lean curs walking dispiritedly behind them, as well as the fact that the mill is frozen up and looks like remaining that way for some time – all these serve to remind us that life's a serious affair. Over everything lies the spellbound silence of a severe Flemish winter's day.

Nothing of Titian's voluptuous countrysides here. This is Northern winter – perhaps its most striking depiction in all art – before which everything must bow. Except perhaps the human spirit. Each of the little towns in the valley has a church, its spire pointing upwards in hope. It is towards these spires that the hunters move. The cold has separated them one from another; they're not talking, but they are heading towards home.

The painting appears to have more in common with Japanese art than with the Italian masters. The strong verticals, supplied by the receding trees which take us into the landscape, the subdued palette – browns, russets, greens, greys – are all tokens of a severe self-discipline controlling the prodigality of vision.

Here is what we most seek in an artist: a universal awareness, to which is coupled an empathy with the human detail.

The comparison between Bruegel and his southern contemporaries is instructive; to appreciate the originality of Bruegel, however, we should note the contrasts between his intentions and those of painters who preceded him.

It happens that about one hundred and fifty years earlier, other artists also left a record of the seasons. *Les Tres Riches Heures du Duc de Berry*, often referred to as *The Book of Hours*, was illustrated and illuminated by more than one artist, working under the direction of the Duc de Berry. It was completed some time after 1416. The most famous section of the book depicts the months of the year. In the twelve months, we observe that people have shadows, and that there are reflections in the water. As far as we know, such representations of natural phenomena had never appeared before.

The bright, clear miniatures of *The Book of Hours* give us a view of medieval life in more than its physical dimension. The peasants toil beneath the castle walls, whatever the season. They are stiff sturdy figures, mere emblems of God's purpose. When nobles appear, gorgeously clad, they are willowy, their hands small, their gestures decorous. The gulf between the two groups is unbridgeable.

Serf or duke, above them looms the castle. Great chateaux dominate the fields and vineyards – and Heaven stands above the chateaux, and there is not a darn thing anyone can do about it. Duke regally welcoming guests to his feast in January, peasants warming their genitals by a fire in February – all are God's creatures, all confined within narrow margins. Hierarchy, and the unthinking obedience hierarchy instils, dominated the Christian mind.

A century and a half later, the varied and lively world of Pieter Bruegel tells another story. We understand what the Renaissance means in terms of the freeing of the spirit of mankind. In the middle of the sixteenth century, when Bruegel was painting, a marked change in climate occurred. From then on, for another century and a half, all parts of the world endured probably the coldest conditions since the end of the last major ice age. *Hunters in the Snow* in fact depicts the onset of the Little Ice Age. Still a more enquiring spirit prevailed. Bruegel celebrates the fact that, although Icarus may have plunged into the sea, he at least aspired and flew.

So we turn from a painting for which one feels profound respect, even awe, to a painting of which I'm fond but cannot help thinking is really rather awful as a painting. It's the sort of picture that demanded the expression 'as pretty as a picture' be coined. We don't think today, as some of our Victorian predecessors did, that pictures and stories need be pretty or improving – mainly, I suppose, because the comforting idea of moral progress has gone down the drain after two world wars.

The Hireling Shepherd, by William Holman Hunt, portrays a rustic scene. There are two human figures in it, a young man and a young woman, and a lot of sheep. The month could be August.

If we know as little about Bruegel as we do about Shakespeare, we know almost too much about William Holman Hunt. He was one of the Pre-Raphaelite Brotherhood; he was born in 1827 and died in 1910, to be buried in Westminster Abbey with due honour. His most famous canvas is *The Light of the World. The Hireling Shepherd* was painted in 1851, the year of the Great Exhibition.

Hunt was an unhappy man; his Christian principles seem to have been at war with his creative impulse. Fame and success brought him little joy.

The Hireling Shepherd is a well-constructed picture, the shepherd and his wench forming a solid triangle, with the girl's head pretty well in the centre of the picture. Parts of the background are attractive and have an airy sense that looks forward to the Impressionists; yet somehow they remain not properly integrated, as if we were looking at spring on the left and high summer on the right. The two country copulatives appear specially dressed for the occasion, like characters in a BBC TV Victorian drama.

The sense of artificiality reinforces the main impression of the painting: that Hunt is not depicting an episode in the everyday life of country-folk, but telling us an improving tale, while standing rather too close to our elbow. The moral appears to be 'When the cat's away, the mice will play.' Only we have sheep instead of mice and while the shepherd is making overtures to the wench, the riotous-looking sheep are getting out of hand, and will soon be despoiling a field of wheat. The lamb on the wench's lap will soon make itself sick on green apples.

Holman Hunt never entirely trusted his paintings to speak for themselves. They did not quite escape from the literary, and a moral had to be added. In this case, our red-faced yokel represents, in Hunt's words, 'The type of muddle-headed pastors, who, instead of performing their services to the flock – which is in constant peril – discuss vain questions of no value to any human soul . . .' Very few today would be reminded of a clergyman by looking at our robust bucolic.

These days, we are less keen to deduce morals, and will probably content ourseves with speculating on what the lad and lass plan to do next on their inviting bank. One curious touch is the death's head moth which the shepherd is trying to show the girl – whether with or without success is for every viewer to decide for himself.

I chose this picture because it is the one I used as a pivotal point in my novel, *Report on Probability A*. The novel – though perfectly easy to read – is often regarded as difficult, because it deals with a situation frozen in time. No unfreezing takes place. Most novels present the reader with a problem to be overcome. The ramifications are carefully built up, we are confronted with a crisis or climax, and then comes resolution. Art copying orgasm. In *Probability A* we have a crisis of a kind, but we never know exactly what kind, since its ramifications are withheld; nor is the situation resolved. This leaves many readers dissatisfied; but a few – those who remain to the end – often receive a heightened sense of time and human drama.

To reinforce the imagery of my suspended situation, a typical nineteenth century painting was needed. My choice was *The Hireling Shepherd*, which I knew well, because it seems to represent in itself the concept of frozen time. In many Victorian pictures, the main interest lies not so much in the composition or the execution or the colour harmony, or in the statement, or even in a way in the actual subject, but in the question we as viewers are forced to ask: *What happens next?* Most Victorian painters were scarcely aware of the existential dilemma, but, living at a time of hectic and unprecedented progress with its concomitant uncertainty, they developed a mode of circumstantial art which managed to make a kind of materialist sense until the question was asked of the canvas, *What happens next?* Why this moment, why not next moment? (Some painters like Augustus Egg, following Hogarth, chose multiple moments and sequential canvasses.)

Although *What happens next?* is a question which expresses uncertainty – mingled anxiety and hope, perhaps – it appeased the anxieties of the Victorians, and does the same for us in our formidable age. The question is not posed, I think, before the nineteenth century, even in the so-called genre pictures of the Dutch school.

The great seventeenth century artist Vermeer painted interiors with ladies reading letters; we take his paintings at their face value, as paintings. To use an old-fashioned word, it would be vulgar to ask of Vermeer, Why this moment, why not next? But a nineteenth century English painting called 'The Letter' is sure to dramatise a situation; there will be clues as to whether someone has died, or a heart has been broken, or a soldier is coming home from the wars, or the mortgage is demanded. The interest is external to the composition. The future is part of the palette. We and the painter ask, *What happens next?* Between Vermeer and Holman Hunt and the two centuries dividing them has come a great change: Change itself. Tomorrow is no longer going to be like the present or the dear dead past. The sheep will be at the corn.

We call the division that brought such change the Industrial Revolution. The first generation to feel that great divide, which separates our modern world from the old

41

lumbering world of mail coaches and infinite leisure, with the squire and parson lording it over the quiet villages – or whatever simplistic images you have of the past – the first generation to feel the pinch of change felt it severely. They were such men as Tennyson, Edgar Allen Poe, Thackeray, Charles Darwin, and Charles Dickens, all born between 1809 and 1812. For them, the railways and railway time-tables arrived. In the works of each of them we can gauge the quickened pulse of change (though we catch that pulse already in Shelley's poems, and in that wonderful novel his second wife wrote).

Thackeray puts it like this:

> We who have lived before railways were made, belong to another world . . . It was only yesterday, but what a gulf between now and then! *Then* was the old world, stage-coaches, more or less swift, riding-horses, pack-horses, highwaymen, knights in armour, Norman invaders, Roman legends, Druids, Ancient Britons painted blue, and so forth – all these belong to the old period . . . But your railroad starts the new era, and we of a certain age belong to the new time and the old one . . . Towards what new continent are we wending? to what new laws, new manners, new politics, vast new expanses of liberties unknown as yet, or only surmised? . . .
>
> We who lived before railways, and survive out of the ancient world, are like Father Noah and his family out of the Ark . . . .

Ever since Thackeray, each generation has experienced similar dislocation. My father suffered in the trenches of World War I. I well recall the dropping of the two atomic bombs on Japan. My children remember the test flights of Concorde, men walking on the Moon. What happens next? All these dislocations are severe, but less severe than the first, because dislocation has become a part of change and change a way of life. All are the result of scientific and technical developments.

Science fiction is a kind of literature springing from the world of change in which we live. It also asks the question, *What happens next?* That was why I used the Holman Hunt picture as a kind of touchstone in *Report on Probability A*. You might find the novel a bit of a riddle, but then the question itself is a bit of a riddle. In many situations, to ask, *What happens next?* is tantamount to asking a more searching question, *What's going on now?*

There are my two pictures. I selected one that is unquestionably great, one that I think rather chocolate-boxy; but I considered both were interesting enough to catch the imagination.

When I was at WBS, a long while ago, I paid great attention to the pictures which then hung in the dining hall. I was astonished to come back, over thirty years later, and find them still hanging there, looking a great deal the worse for wear. There was Hobbema's *Avenue*, a rather ordinary picture which caught my fancy, and several others I recalled. They are moved now, since the hall has been redecorated, but art is important, not least because it can tell you things you don't realise you know until a lot later. It enriches your life by improving your appreciation of the world. The vistas that Bruegel spreads before us represent a terrific imaginative leap, a way of reclassifying the universe. After four centuries the freshness of its vision still has power.

Perhaps you will come back to the school when you

are men and find, with some surprise, that you remember the Bruegel and the Holman Hunt from your days as a boy here – and you may then, with the benefit of another few years, understand them in a different way from my generation.

Perhaps you'll then be able to answer the riddle, *What happens next?*

Grounded in Stellar Art

How do you put a novel together?

So many intuitions and incidents from everyday life go into a novel that they could hardly be listed. Once the writer is launched on a theme with which he is happy, the stray pieces fall into place almost without thought.

Several times, I have attempted a complex novel which was designed to trawl much of what happened to be passing through my mind at the time. Such novels are *The Malacia Tapestry*, *Life in the West*, and the three volumes of *Helliconia*. And, of course, *Bare-foot in the Head*.

Two notorious characters, Ouspensky and Gurdjieff, are talking to each other.

Ouspensky says to the Master, 'Tell me what you think of recurrence. Do we live only this once and then disappear, or does everything repeat and repeat itself, perhaps an endless number of times, only we do not know and do not remember it?'

And Gurdjieff replies, 'The idea of repetition is not the

full and absolute truth, but it is the nearest possible approximation of the truth. In this case, truth can never be expressed in words.' Hedging his bets, as usual.

They're shabby sooth-sayers, O. and G., tippling wine, playing tricks, dossing in old Armenian houses, ending up whipping Katherine Mansfield in Fontainebleu. O. and G. are the first hippie philosophers, and as such ideal models for the psycho-blasted Europe portrayed in *Barefoot*. They took over a bit as I wrote. Their confident expectation of the miraculous, their quest for it, their finding of it in everyday life, on railway platforms, in steamy cafés, in the suburbs of our pleasure, is very attractive. Maybe it's more fun to go in search of the miraculous than the truth. As Charteris does.

That having been said, the idea of the eternal return is a horrifying one. It fuels the most alarming episode in *Barefoot*, 'The Serpent of Kundalini'.

A novel is like a dream in that it is not a linear event, although the events within it may be described later by critics in a linear way. When we stand back and hold a novel up to the light of day, it reveals many dimensions. *Barefoot in the Head* was built to display many dimensions, that being one of its themes.

Here's a dimension the critics might not think of. When the novel was launched in England, its dust jacket bore two prices, one in old currency, one in new. Thus: 30s. / £1.50. The times trembled like reeds in rippled water. What critics make of the novel is inevitably less than the novel. Each critic angles his or her interest, brings up different coloured fish. James Joyce scholars find that Ouspensky meets Joyce.

Scholars weaned on music and drugs will find, I ween,

music and drugs. European critics fish out the connection between Jugoslavia and the rest of Europe.

The beginnings of the book were indeed Joycean. Driving through the night in that confused region of Europe where France, Belgium and Holland comprise one large *laager*, where the Meuse becomes the Maars, I saw a broken neon sign flaring purple in the dark. STELLA ART it said. In fact, the name of the lager is Stella Artois, but I drank to Stellar Art. I forgot the first half of a French bird. In the mood of the sixties, with all possibilities possible, the sign started amazing wings of thought in my crane. The Meuse and the Maars, the same river under different names, symbolised the changing stream of Europe's many paths.

A united Europe, united in the chaos of LSD, the drug then conquering the world. An automatic culture of the automobile. Under the influence of mescalin, which has a structural biochemical relationship with LSD, Aldous Huxley saw a car. 'A large pale blue automobile was standing at the kerb. At the sight of it, I was suddenly overcome by enormous merriment. What complacency, what an absurd self-satisfaction beamed from those bulging surfaces of glossiest enamel! Man had created the thing in his own image . . . I laughed till the tears ran down my cheeks.'

A touch of caricature was all I needed. For the future had alighted in the mid-sixties, and everything was an exaggerated version of its old self. That was true for me too. At a time of greatest happiness, I had vision. The great public world was my secret, and I travelled it openly.

Was Western culture, the 'Westciv' of the book, going down the great water-closet of history, and I alone privy to it?

This business of language. A novelist's problems are not a critic's. I wanted to talk about my acid heads, and I could see no other way to get close to them than to copy their thought and speech patterns. But what I was doing was boning up on Europe, not on James Joyce. I wrote from life, not books – give a man enough Europe and he will hack himself. I wanted to diagnose out the actual situation developing. People came to me and said, 'You're not writing about what the future will be like, Brian, you're writing about what it's like around Europe now.' I jotted down notes for the novel in Belgium and the Netherlands and France and Germany and Italy and up in the Scandinavian countries. And in Loughborough. I stayed in the hotel in Metz which features in the 'Just Passing Through' episode.

The confusion of language parallels the confusion of landscape as well as the confusion in the minds of Charteris & Co.

I'm a bit sceptical about having this Joyce thing hung on me. James Blish, a confirmed Joycean, started it. He carried on at great length about the language of the novel; I said, 'Yes, Jim, but the language is about something.'

Of course there are some good puns. Vaginisthmus of Panamama. Dungeoness. Agenbite of Auschwitz. Etc. The groundlings must be amused. But such matters, and such sportiveness with language, are not unique to this book. For instance, a discerning critic picked out the one sentence in *Barefoot* which appears also in *Report on Probability A*.

All authors who write half-way literate English owe much to few writers, to Shakespeare, Johnson, and – if you are going to remint the coinage – James Joyce. But we have such a flexible tongue. The game's infinite and easy as walking, that learned instinct. I think therefore I amble.

There are parallels between Joyce's 'Old mutther-goosip' and *Barefoot*'s 'Old Mumma Goosetale'; but there are so many associations to words. Goose: a silly girl, a tailor's iron; geese saved the Capitol, you go to goose fairs, goose month was the lying-in month for women; the Nazis did the goose step; there are geese you can't say Boo to, and others that lay golden eggs; there is also the royal game of goose, which I assume you play with women. But more important to the story and to the instance of 'Old Mumma Goosetale' is the fact that the goose is Angeline's pet bird – it comforted her when she was sad as a child. The language is not there for its own sweet sake, but for the effects it generates.

Page 92. 'He gave a sort of half-laugh by a wall, his beard growing in its own silence.' Perfect English, perfect sentence. One of the best I ever wrote. When I'd got that sentence down, I knocked off for the rest of the day.

I tried to convey confusion as clearly as I could.

You would possibly get more mileage by comparing this novel with my other novels than with *Finnegans Wake*. As the Irishman said, 'Sure, I couldn't rade it in a wake of Sondays.' One device I used was not contracted or even expanded from Joyce, the insertion of holophrastic words – using a single extant word to express a complex of ideas. An example is on page 137: 'The Serb had ceased to think what he was saying. It was the migratory converse.' Here, 'converse' can mean either 'conversation' or the converse of conversation. Which is a way of expressing the war within Charteris's mind; he is not thinking with his conscious brain but with his cerebellum, from the Latin 'cera', wax, and 'bellum', war – a war waxing and John Wayning in the skull.

I intended this confusion of language to be more a fusion than a con.

49

I took more from Ouspensky than from Joyce, more from Baedeker than from *Ulysses*. One critic, hooked on Joyce, came up with a car called 'Leopold II' as a tribute to Bloom. The reference is to page 176; that's where this phantom vehicle appears: 'Tumultaneously, the broad Leopold II sloughed its pavements for grey sand and cliffs cascated up where buildings were.' It shows what a clever commentator can read into a book. But in Brussels there's a broad highway called Leopold II; it is named to honour not literature but the King of the Belgians.

Through this monster plan of mindpattern comes the serpent, the serpent of Kundalini, an ancient conservative Hindu force rising from the older tributories of the brain into the neocortex. This primitivism has to fuse with the new world of speed and motorways. It is an energy Gurdjieff believed in, which he tried to flog into Katherine Mansfield, Aldous Huxley, and the other fashionables who visited his clinic at Fontainebleu. The energy is in Charteris, but we may believe he masks it by changing his name from the Serbian 'Dushan' to Charteris, the writer of the Saint stories. He comprehends the multiplicity of I's, of which Gurdjieff speaks.

Ancient wisdom has to be transmitted to man's higher centres. *Barefoot* embraces the eternal return. The first Charteris dies on reaching England, in Brontosaurus Broadway, detained by philosophy and love and a dose of Glen Miller. He asks a final question, 'Cannot one act *and* dream?' (page 49). And that is what the next Charteris does, acts and dreams, mainly in England, the land of his dreams. We can never be sure whether the 'real' Charteris did not remain in Serbia. Is this literally 'his imagined England'? (page 28). We may be dealing only with a multiplicity of cast-off I's, rather like the multiplicity of universes in *Report on Probability A*.

But, as Charteris says, '*Here* is the permanent position' (page 260), provided 'you hold fast to dreamament.' My own feelings enter the novel at this point, focussed on the notion of eternal return. Much of life is dreamament. It is enough to *be*. Christian ethics form no part of Charteris's thinking; fortified by the psychochemicals, he sees only 'the infinite points of intersection' (page 246). Because of this – almost too late – he refuses the cross, which he perhaps regards as a Crucifiction.

But demented Europe still clings to the Judeo-Christian ethos; it's 'the old worn Westciv groove'. Saviours are part of a big cliché in the sky. If Charteris is to be a real saviour, Cass is ready as Judas, and Charteris is in line for the Cross. That is further down the line than he is prepared to go.

He becomes more of a saint by ceasing to play the Saint, and opts for a quieter way of life, in conformity with Gurdjieff's dictum, 'As long as a man takes himself as one person he will never move from where he is.'

A raddled pastoral follows. 'All the known noon world loses its staples and everything drops apart.' At least one of Charteris's alternative I's can alter native thought and live peacefully to be ninety, revered by all but Angeline. Eternal recurrence ends the book, with forests dwindling again and new travellers blowing in from the north. The laws of energy see to that.

Although self-improvement is a crooked trail, Charteris gets somewhere. He learns to notice neglected Angeline, whom he has sometimes in the past carelessly called Angelina, as if even her name was a matter of indifference. Angeline is an important figure. She remains constant and stays with Charteris, although he has killed her husband. Then 'she broke with elmed summer into twain' and bore him a child; this marks a new independence for her.

The last Charteris we see achieves love instead of his previous self-centredness, and some perception of the woman. She is 'no longer the greylagging little girl' she used to be. Angeline complains a lot in old age. As he goes out, near death, to speak to the disciples, he recalls how he loved her, 'loved her in my way loved her being in many women,' and attempts in awkward fashion to tell her as much. Bent double, muddled, gnarled, confused, he can only say when she wakes, 'I had a little speech for you.' Angeline, cross and ancient, ticks him off. 'Heard too many of your speeches in my time.' She would have no time for Molly Bloom's monologue.

With the self-improvement comes more self-knowledge. As the disciples wait under the final tree, Charteris plays a last crafty Gurdjieffian trick. 'He would give them holy law okay but spiced with heresy.' And he pronounces the sentence which every reader must riddle for himself, 'All possibilities and alternatives exist but ultimately – ultimately you want it both ways.'

Perhaps what is represented is a human inability to verbalise the deepest things – the very barrier *Barefoot* tries so hard to transcend through its prose and its integral poems.

As for memory, it is an enemy to new lives. (The spirit of the sixties itself failed, and we were doomed to live through the stonier seventies and eighties, replaying the old records.) The old life does not digest. Charteris is always conscious of his father, the good old Serbian Communist, his death and his funeral. These images come back from another time, another land. 'My capital crime nostalgia.' So similarly Angeline dreams of her lost garden, befriended by geese.

From such seminal memories there is no waking, just as the psychochemicals do not provide the forward evolutionary thrust for which some hope but rather reproduce a Neanderthal vagueness of thought. The physiology brings fuzzy ologies.

It seems as if nothing of the old Westciv way of life survives – except the Head, from whence come all capital offences. There's a golden glow over the decay, laced with the irony of the final paradox, which would surely appeal to Gurdjieff: 'Keep violence in the mind where it belongs.'

There is an aspiration to higher consciousness. But ultimately this must rest with the reader.

It Takes Time to Tango

The absurdities of history are well illustrated in the case of the western attitude to China. A deadly enemy at one time, China changed overnight to everyone's favourite Communist country – 'the glory, jest, and riddle of the world'.

The story of how President Richard Nixon made contact with Chairman Mao, at least as that story is told in the memoirs of Henry Kissinger, is a remarkable piece of modern day fantasy in itself. Kissinger's mission to Peking was so secret that he flew to Pakistan, feigned a cold, and retired to the President of Pakistan's mountain retreat. There a Chinese plane was awaiting him. His escort pulled their guns on Kissinger; their orders were that he should travel in no kind of vehicle not made in the USA and not driven or piloted by a military man with full security clearance. Kissinger out-talked his guard and they all climbed into the cramped plane. That night in Peking, when Kissinger was in his pavilion in the Forbidden City, there came a knock at his door. Enter one of the most remarkable men of our century: Chou En Lai. And the talking began.

Within a few months, Richard Nixon was walking the Great Wall of China, and everyone was falling over themselves a) to say nice things about the hitherto hated Chinese, and b) to get to China, preferably at someone else's expense.

I found a) easy, since I had always admired the Chinese. By a bit of luck, b) fell into my lap also. So, at an interesting moment, when China was once more avid for breezes from outside, I became part of a special historical process. A plane carried me over the Himalayas from Islamabad on roughly the same course that Kissinger had followed, and, in October 1979, I found myself on Chinese soil in a state of wild excitement. After all those years, it had proved possible to visit another planet.

Kunming is a pleasant city to the south of China, with a climate of perpetual spring. There are good buildings and a sense of leisure. Only two hundred miles away is the Burmese frontier. It was evening, after sunset, and I strolled into Kunming Park.

A line of twenty-five watt bulbs burned above one of the walks. Beneath the dim lights, a crowd of young people was gathering. Some were dancing to the music of a wind-up gramophone. Old ten-inch records were being played. Couples were tangoing.

So the repercussions of the Cultural Revolution became manifest. It was not simply Beethoven who had been banned. Guy Lombardo and Edmundo Ross had also gone to the wall.

Yet here was Guy, here was Edmundo again, giving out under the mild night sky, as if the Twenties had never passed away. The old records had not been smashed, or the old rhythms forgotten, despite a million Little Red Books. No

South American ever did a smoother tango than those Chinese. Six of them would share the local equivalent of a 7-Up while others danced in the limited space. They did not need alcohol; they had happiness. The dull visibility did not dim their beautiful spirits. They were young and free and all things were possible.

I'll never forget that tango. China was full of items I had never thought of before. Every day a fresh surprise. Courtesy. Mountains. Beautiful spiders on a flower-bed full of giant French marigolds and cactus. Close-up view of a hysterectomy undergone with acupuncture anaesthesia. The Ming tombs. Calligraphy. Standing beneath the gate from which the silk caravans once left for Trebizond and Bokhara. The taste of persimmons. The impossible questions we asked the Chinese. The impossible questions they asked us: 'What precisely is the difference between American and English literatures?'

Travel is a perverse passion. Why do we leave home, with its comforts and routines, and subject ourselves to the indignities of airlines? Why, to enjoy discomfort and broken routine elsewhere. In many ways, I am an easy customer to satisfy when abroad; I just want something to go wrong.

Nothing went wrong in China – the reverse, in fact – but the prospect remained. At Xian airport, a storm grounded planes for a while. When I told a chap in the bar (well, it wasn't a bar actually, but that's another story) that I was flying to Kunming he pulled a face and said, 'That'll mean an Ilyushin 18. Lousy old planes. They're always crashing nose first. The Chinese keep the first six rows of seats empty to lower the casualty rate.'

I thought of these words as we crossed the tarmac to board our delayed flight. There, in CAAC insignia, stood an aged turboprop. It was an Ilyushin 18. These machines had been acquired from the Soviets in the nineteen-fifties, before the USSR and China fell out with each other. Aboard, a hostess brings you sweets and fizzy mineral water, and all the passengers wear green. The seats are canvas.

Once we were airborne, I evaded the hostess's detaining arm, went forward and peered round the curtain to where the first class seating should have been. There stood six rows of empty seats, shrouded in white, the Chinese colour for death.

So it was true. After thirty years of arduous service, the turboprop was due for a crash at any time.

The Chinese admit they are short of various sorts of transport. They also appear to be short of roads. Shortages of roads and vehicles in all provinces form a severe obstacle to increasing tourism and exports. The China any visitor sees is limited by this factor as much as by political calculation.

So you may find yourself faced with the prospect of a forty-eight hour train journey. Seize it. You will never have a rarer experience. By rail, one gains a faint notion of the scale of Chinese distances, the scenery is good to amazing, and the dining car stays open all day. The car attendant doubles as barefoot doctor.

The train stops occasionally at very long deserted stations. Everyone gets out. Hard class has a wash in long stone troughs provided on the platforms. Old ladies sell cakes, fruit, and bread. One stares through locked station gates at a peaceful village in the middle of nowhere which one will never see again. A mother plays ball with her child; one cannot wait long enough to see how the little game ends. An English lady asks a peasant through an interpreter, 'But are you really happy in China, *really* happy?'

Once we stopped at Chang-Sha, and were taken to visit

a museum which featured a long dead Bronze Age princess, naturally mummified. We looked down on her; she was withered but tranquil, and her reproductive organs were separately displayed. Nearby was a perfect crossbow made in 1860 BC.

Oh, there were plenty of marvels, large and small. Large: the Great Wall, greater than can be imagined; the so-called Buried Army, where six thousand terracotta soldiers of the first Emperor of China march out of the soil to a daylight they have not visited for two thousand years. Small: a bed where Chou En Lai slept before the Revolution; schoolgirls we met in a Peking park, when asked what they wanted for their birthdays – no, no make-up sets, no CB radios – longingly, they said 'Pens and paper.'

But the most marvellous thing, if you discount the light itself and the wondrous politico-geographical fact of yourself actually standing on Chinese soil, is the Chinese people. Particularly in country districts men and women look at you and smile with genuine friendship – don't they? They give you something. They are multitudinous humanity. They are confident, yet no more aggressive than deer. In such a peaceful country, the terrors of the past are hard to believe.

And they speak of those terrors without malice. An artist was beaten up by Red Guards. He lay wounded in a gutter. No one dared go to his aid. But a dog ran over to him and licked his face. Seeing this, a Red Guard dashed up and killed the dog with one blow. Since then, the artist, now recovered, paints only animals. Animals don't suffer from ideology, a more deadly malady than rabies.

The people are long-suffering. 'Eat bitterness,' small children are taught. Suffer and endure. Most lives are lived on very little, captains of industry earn £15 per week. Villages at night are dark, almost unlit. During an interview with Vice-Premier Deng Xiao Ping, I watched him smile slyly as he pointed out the spittoon by his chair. 'I'm the last head of state to use one of those,' he said. 'I'm just a countryman . . . You probably earn four times as much as I do.'

This poverty has a transcendant quality, different from, for instance, the Stone Age poverty prevailing in parts of India. Despite periodic madnesses, China is a well-run country, and run for the poor, since there are only poor. Many of the production brigades, with their shared incentives, were admirable, though they are now being absorbed into larger units. It would be wonderful to think that China might solve problems which still confront the rest of the world. Better that than that China should follow some half-cocked Western model, as Mao followed Marxism. The future lies as thick – and as enigmatic – as does the past over Deng's domain.

All one can say is – go and see for yourself: China is different. People's expectations are different. In three weeks, you can feel that difference in your bones. You may not be able to express it, but you will never forget it. And it may make a difference in you.

Robert Sheckley's World: Australia

Travel does not merely broaden the mind. Sometimes it lengthens it.

That is certainly the case if you fly from England to Australia. By one of those primitive old Boeing 747s, it takes about twenty hours instead of the ninety minutes any reasonably minded sf reader would expect. Time passes with preternatural sloth, marked only by one plastic tray full of food following another like the flapping of a great bat's wing. One tries to read. Here at last is the heaven-sent chance to digest *Moby Dick* . . . But concentration and the stratosphere are enemies. One tries to recite silently one's favourite poems, or at least the poems one remembers, which rarely happen to be one's favourites.

At Flores in the Azores Sir Richard Grenville lay . . .

But the words twist and distort themselves, turning into hitherto unknown nonsense versions of nursery rhymes.

Pease pudding hot, pease pudding cold,
I'm in the parlour clock, half-past mould.

What does it mean? One arrives at destination in a sur-realist frame of mind. Which is just as well if the destination is Australia.

Australia was something of an eye-opener. From Singapore, the plane flew straight till it was over Darwin. It then turned right a bit and spent several hours suspended over utter desolation. Have you noticed that about desolation? It is always either utter or unutterable?

Very little had ever happened down there and very little ever could. The very processes of creation had been skimped. Passengers looked down in horror, bar sales rocketed. Jerry-built people in a jerry-built world.

My mind, like a caged bird seized by a terror or a touch of the trots, darted back a million years, then forward a million years. As it banged its little feathered breast against the cage of centuries, all it could visualise was flash floods followed by droughts, flash floods followed by droughts, flash floods followed by droughts, and so on, punctuated only by inundations and dry spells. Bar sales rocketed again, reaching a new highball.

It made you ashamed to be an Earthman. What would aliens think of this cutprice planet?

After some hours of this mind-mincing nothingness, the plane achieved a point over Alice Springs. There the legendary city was, two miles below us: numerous tiny roofs and a bar or two, with outer defences of broken-down car bodies. Singapore Airlines took a half-left turn for the worse. Before you could say 'Emergency Oxygen Equipment', we were dawdling over the Simpson Desert, several hundred million years back in the past, before life was patented.

Topography reached its nadir. What was that stuff down there? No general geographical term applied; it wasn't a desert or plain or savannah or steppe. No, a new term had to be invented for it, an essentially Australian term. The Outback. Up went the bar sales again.

By the time we landed in Sydney, to confront the new terrors of blue gums and toy koalas made from genuine kangaroo fur, I had twigged. The truth dawned. This was Sfland. I had been transferred to a planet designed by Robert Sheckley. Who else could have invented the Australian continent with all its implausibilities? The author of *Dimension of Miracles* had been at work here.

I suppose it was this sense of the extraordinary which made my trip so memorable. Frankly, I was surprised to find ordinary congenial human beings living in the place. Well, I say ordinary . . . I did notice a tendency on the part of the population of Sydney to grab any passing Pommie, drag him to the Heads of that celebrated harbour, and point eastwards across the ocean, asking, 'Do you know what the nearest city is?' Pause, two, three – then their answer to their own rhetorical question: 'Valpar-bloody-aiso, seven thousand, two hundred and sixteen miles away.'

Once, I took the liberty of pointing in the opposite direction and enquiring the name of the nearest city to the west. Here the ordinary citizens were less sure of their facts. One said 'Canberra,' and fell to the ground weeping, where he was quickly eaten by a passing platypus. (Ah, we travellers could tell some tales . . .)

Once I was with two ordinary citizens, and, in crazed response to my question, they fell to quarrelling.

'Perth,' one said.

'Dar-es-Salaam,' said the other, 'you stupid git!'

'No, Perth's much nearer.'

'No, Dar-es-Salaam is nearer – about five thousand miles nearer.' The argument came to blows. Which was embarrasing, since they had been engaged for a week only. In the end, the girl won on a technical knockout.

Wherever I went, I found the same obsession with distance. I can say without contradiction that, in the minds of its inhabitants, Australia is the biggest country in this or any other Sheckley-inspired nightmare. No matter where you go, it's always nearer to Dar-es-Salaam. Chris Priest, when staying in Melbourne, was invited to give a talk at a small school in Noojee or Nagambie or Bininyong, or one of those places about a hundred miles outside Melbourne with names that make us roar with laughter in Ashby-de-la-Zouche, Budleigh Salterton or Maidenhead. The teacher lady introducing Chris to the class said, 'And our guest has come a really long, long way to be here with us this morning. We're very grateful to him, since we've never had the privilege of a visit from someone from that part of the world before. So let's give a warm welcome to Mr Priest, who has made it all the way from Melbourne to be with us.'

I bypassed Noojee and Nagambie to take in the science fiction convention in Melbourne. It was all I had been led to expect, except for the general shortage of drink and the amazing number of teetotallers attending. Also attending was a party from Perth. Because of religious and political objections, they had decided not to fly. So they spent five days on the train and six on camels, polishing off the last hundred miles by yak and wallaby.

They were splendid people. I said to one, 'Perth's a bit far from anywhere, I gather.'

'Too bloody near Dar-es-Salaam for my liking,' he said.

As the contours of our bodies are shaped by the skeletons trapped inside, so, it seems, is the Australian psyche shaped by the alien geology of the country. A bizarre quality prevails over the most innocent landscape, reminding the visitor that he treads ancient Gondwanaland, and that time must still be – somewhere, secretly – early Paleozoic. This sense of a brutal landscape untrodden by the classical gods is well conveyed in Patrick White's marvellous novel, *A Fringe of Leaves*, in which Mrs Roxborough, an English lady visiting Australia at the beginning of the last century, is shipwrecked on the Queensland coast and captured by aborigines. It is a novel choked with the harsh Australian version of nature.

Of course the Australian psyche is also haunted by a sense of transplantation to alien soil. The effect can be felt in North America, but never so strongly as in Australia. It is not simply that Australia was once used as a dumping ground for British criminals; the Indians of North America were practically wiped out by the colonists, whereas in Australia one is constantly aware of the aborigines, displaced, dispossessed, despairing. A sense of ancient past cheek-by-jowl with raw newness does not easily fade.

To visit Australia is to understand in a small way the difficulties which would attend the establishment of a colony on an alien planet.

This prevailing wind from the past is soon forgotten when one is sitting talking to the sf fraternity Down Under. Their preoccupations are the same as elsewhere.

The old teasing relationship with England pops up only occasionally.

Lee Harding is one of the most interesting sf writers Down Under. In his fiction, he frequently tries to come to terms with the particular burden of the past which is Australia's. An excellent example is his novel *Waiting for the End of the World* (1983), in which the main character, who lives in the Australia of the next century, is haunted by visitors from a remote past. Lee and his wife, Irene, took me out to their place in the Dandenong Ranges to the north of Melbourne, a beautiful spot filled with all the varieties of gum tree you could or could not name.

One day, we were walking through the forest which encroaches on Lee's back door. We followed a winding track among the trees. As we got to a wooden bridge over a dried gully, I looked down into the gully and said, casually, 'Oh, look, Lee, there's a lyre bird. And there's another one over there.'

Lee and Irene almost fell over. He had walked in this forest for twenty years and had never seen a lyre bird. To me, they were part of the stock repertory of odd Australian fauna, like wallabies and koala bears. Lee knew, as I did not, how scarce the birds were.

Deeper in the forest, we were surrounded by ferns and cycads. The very sounds in the air seemed different, the intensity of the light was different. Again came the feeling of being overtaken by something ancient. I said something of the sort to Lee. My exact words came up at me from the printed page when – several years later – I read a copy of *Waiting for the End of the World* and got to page 9, where those words are printed in italics. That was the way Lee played a time-trick on me, and built me into his book. Not for the first time, I felt like a plaything in *Dimension of Miracles*.

The Sheckley Effect was still working.

In Nicholas Roeg's marvellous Australian movie *Walkabout* a lost girl and her little brother consort with aborigines and in particular with an aborigine boy. The sister, played by Jenny Agutter, comes to realise when returned to civilisation that the richest part of her life had been when she was lost in the wilderness with the aborigine who died for love of her. Nevertheless, she must live out the rest of her days in cities. That is her destiny.

Mrs Roxborough, in Patrick White's novel, comes to the same perception but, as it were, from the opposite viewpoint. She is lying in filth in a low hut, the slave of an aborigine, naked but for the fringe of leaves. She thinks of her previous existence in England.

She realised that most of her life at Cheltenham had been a bore and that she might only have experienced happiness while scraping carrots, scouring pails, or lifting the clout to see whether the loaves were proved.

Since so much of Australia is almost uncreated, almost uninhabitable, it provokes such thoughts. Those thoughts never lie comfortable, as Mrs Roxborough lay comfortable beside the dead fire in the hut. They remind us that we are prisoners inside whatever freedoms we enjoy. They remind us that humanity did a deal long ago, when, with spear and bow-and-arrow and the first flickerings of technology, men decided to separate themselves from the encompassing natural world. This was what Christians would term The

Fall. They remind us that we have lost something; however fast 747s fly, they do not let us escape our domesticated selves.

They remind us that Australia is not just a place you fly to via Singapore Airlines. It is also a state of mind. However far we travel, we are stuck with it. Brains have taproots into the soil.

If God had intended us to think, surely he would have provided us with cut-off switches?

Sheckley, you've got a lot to answer for.

Sturgeon: Mercury Plus X

Sturgeon? The name was magnetic. There it was, perpetually cropping up attached to the stories I most admired. Sturgeon: quite an ordinary Anglo-American word among exotics like A.E. Van Vogt, Isaac Asimov, Heinlein, Simak, and Kuttner. Yet – spiky, finny, odd. And it was not his original name. Theodore Hamilton Sturgeon was born Edward Hamilton Waldo. To the usual boring, undeserving parents. That was on Staten Island, the year the First World War ended.

So there were two of him, as there are of many a good writer. A bright side, a dark side – much like our old sf image of Mercury, remember, so much more interesting than banal reality. He had a mercurial temperament.

The bright side was the side everybody loved. There was something so damned nice, charming, open, empathic, and elusive about Ted that women flocked to him. Men too. Maybe he was at the mercy of his own fey sexuality. If so, he was quizzical about it, as about everything. One of his more cutesy titles put it admirably: 'If All Men Were Brothers,

Would You Let One Marry Your Sister?' Not if it was Sturgeon, said a too-witty friend.

He played his guitar. He sang. He shone. He spoke of his philosophy of love.

Ted honestly brought people happiness. If he was funny, it was a genuine humour which sprang from seeing the world aslant. A true sf talent. Everyone recognised his strange quality – 'faunlike', some nut dubbed it; faunlike he certainly looked. Inexplicable, really.

Unsympathetic stepfather, unsatisfactory adolescence. Funny jobs, and 'Ether Breather' out in *Astounding* in 1939. So to an even funnier job, science fiction writer. It's flirting with disaster.

I could not believe those early stories: curious subject matter, bizarre resolutions, glowing style. And about sexuality. You could hardly believe your luck when one of Ted's stories went singing through your head.

'It', with Cartier illustrations, in *Unknown*. Terrifying. 'Derm Fool'. Madness. The magnificent 'Microcosmic God', read and re-read. 'Killdozer', appearing after a long silence. There were to be other silences. 'Baby is Three': again in the sense of utter incredibility with complete conviction, zinging across a reader's synapses. By a miracle, the blown-up version, *More Than Human*, was no disappointment either. This was Sturgeon's caviar dish. Better even than *Venus Plus X* with its outré sexuality in a hermaphrodite utopia.

As for those silences. Something sank Sturgeon. His amazing early success, his popularity with fans and stardom at conventions – they told against the writer. Success is a vampire. In the midst of life we are in definite trouble. They say Sturgeon was the first author in the field ever to sign a six-book contract. A six-book contract was a rare mark of distinction, like being crucified. A mark of extinction. Ted was no stakhanovite and the deal did for him; he was reduced to writing a novelisation of a schlock TV series, *Voyage to the Bottom of the Sea*, to fulfil his norms.

At one time, he was reduced further to writing TV pilot scripts for Hollywood. He lived in motels or trailers, between marriages, between lives. Those who read *The Dreaming Jewels* or *Venus Plus X* or the story collections forget that writing is secretly a heavy load, an endless battle against the disappointments which come from within as well as without – and reputation a heavier load. Ted was fighting his way back to the light when night came on.

About Ted's dark side.

Well, he wrote that memorable novel, *Some of Your Blood*, about this crazy psychotic who goes for drinking menstrual discharge. Actually, it does not taste as bad as Ted made out. That was his bid to escape the inescapable adulation.

One small human thing he did. He and I, with James Gunn, were conducting the writers' workshop at the Conference of the Fantastic at Boca Raton, Florida. This was perhaps three years ago.

Our would-be writers circulated their effusions around the table for everyone's comment. One would-be was a plump, pallid, unhappy lady. Her story was a fantasy about a guy who tried three times to commit suicide, only to be blocked each time by a green monster from Hell who wanted him to keep on suffering. Sounds promising, but the treatment was hopeless.

Dumb comments around the table. I grew impatient with their unreality. When the story reached me, I asked the lady right out, 'Have you ever tried to commit suicide?'

Unexpected response. She stared at me in shock. Then she burst into a hailstorm of tears, collapsing onto the table. 'Three times,' she cried. Everyone looked fit to faint.

'It's nothing to be ashamed of,' I said. 'I've tried it too.'

'So have I,' said Sturgeon calmly.

He needen't have come in like that. He just did it bravely, unostentatiously, to support me, to support her, to support everyone. And I would guess there was a lot of misery and disappointment in Ted's life, for all the affection he generated. Yet he remained kind, loving, giving. (The lady is improving by the way. We're still in touch. That's another story.)

If that does not strike you as a positive story, I'm sorry. I'm not knocking suicide, either. Everyone should try it at least once.

Ted was a real guy, not an idol, an effigy, as some try to paint him. He was brilliant, so he suffered. I know beyond doubt that he would be pleased to see me set down some of the bad times he had. He was not one to edit things out. Otherwise he would have been a less powerful writer.

There are troves of lovely Sturgeon tales (as in the collection labelled *E Pluribus Unicorn*), like 'Bianca's Hands', which a new generation would delight in. He wrote well, if sometimes over-lushly. In many ways, Ted was the direct opposite of the big technophile names of his generation, like Doc Smith, Poul Anderson, Robert Heinlein, et al. His gaze was more closely fixed on people. For that we honoured him, and still honour him. Good for him that he never ended up in that prick's junkyard where they pay you a million dollars advance for some crud that no sane man wants to read.

Ted died early in May in Oregon, of pneumonia and other

complications. Now he consorts with Sophocles, Phil Dick, and the author of the *Kama Sutra*. He had returned from a holiday in Hawaii, taken in the hopes he might recover his health there. That holiday, incidentally, was paid for by another sf writer – one who often gets publicity for the wrong things. Thank God, there are still some good guys left. We are also duly grateful for the one just departed.

The Glass Forest

We can draw a clear line at the point where life begins. The expulsion from the womb marks our entry into the world. Where a life-story begins is less clear. So mine will open with the Tea Vision. The Tea Vision marked a first awareness that I enjoyed an interior life apparently not communicable to others.

I was three years old. Our living room, high above our shop, had large windows and comfortable window seats, from which one could look out at the people coming and going in Norwich Street. Opposite was the grocers, Kingston & Hurn. In the upper windows, my 'Aunt' Nellie Hurn could be glimpsed occasionally, living out her life in velvets, playing patience behind her clicking bead curtains.

In the shop windows below, Nellie's husband installed an advert for Mazawattee Tea, based on *Alice in Wonderland* characters. There sat Alice, at the head of the table, pouring Mazawattee tea from a huge red pot into cups which the Mad Hatter and the March Hare were holding. Beaming with pleasure, they lifted the cups to their mouths to drink.

When they lowered the cups, the cups were immediately refilled. No pause in the action was permitted. In those days the design would be solidly made of three-ply and worked off the electric mains.

Passers-by in the street watched the advert for a moment, smiled and walked on. I was its captive. I could not stop observing from my window. The pleasures of the Mad Hatter and the March Hare never dimmed. Their smiles never grew less. The teapot never emptied. They never had too much Mazawattee Tea.

Only in the early morning, before Kingston's opened at 8:00, were they still, Alice with the teapot poised, the others smiling in anticipation.

I truly feared the Mazawattee Tea advert. It introduced me to metaphysical horror. I 'knew' these creatures could not have feelings. And yet – why not? They had movement, smiles, appetites, the appurtenances of feelings. *Who knew I had feelings?*

From such infantile questionings, much follows. I always wanted to find out, always wanted to know the truth.

Our shop – the shop known in bold lettering facing up Norwich Street as H. H. Aldiss – is gone. We left it long ago. Yet it is there that everything must begin. All the trails lead back to H. H. Aldiss.

When my Aunt Dorothy died in the late spring of 1984, she had delivered back much of my life to me. A life story cannot be said to start with birth or end with death. Mine is a jigsaw which might as well continue with Dorothy's modest funeral.

Dorothy Aldiss left her last wish in my wife's and my care. She wanted to be buried beside her husband, who had died back in 1937. No one could have been more devoted to a husband's memory than she; and through her I had come to love the tough old man.

Auntie lived near us in Oxford. The family grave lay across the country, in East Dereham, in the dull heart of Norfolk where I had been born. From long distance, Margaret and I arranged gravediggers, parsons, undertakers, and a firm of stonemasons to heave the marble cross off the mouldering remains of my grandfather and his first wife and to prepare for a new incumbent.

But my aunt was no blood relation. She was my grand-father's second wife. They married in 1930, when he was seventy and she some thirty years his junior. The family was furious; they saw their inheritance threatened.

The funeral was private. I said a few words of valediction. I had become the head of our small family. We then ate lunch in Dereham's one acceptable restaurant, after which we left the town forever – or forever as far as I was concerned.

Dorothy was ninety-five when she died. She had a dry sense of humour and never told a story twice. She remained compos mentis until the last fortnight of her life. She wished I was the son she never had.

The man Auntie married late in his life was Harry Hildyard Aldiss. He hailed from Horncastle in Lincolnshire, where my father, Stanley Aldiss, was born. As a young man, H. H. went to Dereham and bought an ailing draper's business. He was a stocky man of great force of character. No one trifled with him, but he was just and had a quick wit. He was respected by his staff, which numbered nearly fifty as the firm prospered. His sons called him 'Guv'ner'.

H. H. became a big name in East Dereham, and a J. P.

He was a devout Congregationalist, so that Congregational-
ism became the creed we all followed. We had our own
family pews in the William Cowper Memorial Church in
the market square, and were not allowed to look at the stills
outside the nearby cinema when we escaped from the church
services. God was not in favour of Hollywood, or card-
playing, or drink, though he made, in his mercy, an exception for elderberry wine.

My grandfather's success in business probably owed much
to his teetotalism – not a noted characteristic in the Aldiss
family. Indeed, one etymological dictionary derives Aldiss as
a corruption of 'Alehouse', which says much about our
ancestors.

The Aldisses have been in Norfolk for many generations.
When I was bookselling, I came across a slender pamphlet
detailing the names of those who had contributed to the
Defence of the Realm Against the Spanish Armada. One John
Aldis, yeoman of East Anglia, had contributed a sheep and
a farthing. For centuries, the family fortunes have scarcely
varied, sandwiched between peasants and the squirearchy,
neither dying out nor overrunning the county, as rabbits did
in my boyhood. Ours are the middle parts of fortune. Her
privates we.

My grandfather was the son of a seventh son of a seventh
son. All the earlier sons went to sea. One, I know, in the
middle of last century, caught a fatal fever aboard ship, and
was buried at sea off Newfoundland. My grandfather stayed
on dry land. But every Christmas we gave him a book on
his hero, Scott of the Antarctic, if a new study was to be
found.

One day travelling home to Dereham on the train from
Norwich, H. H. got into conversation with a man who was

trying to sell his house. H. H. showed interest. The man described it. 'I know the place,' said H. H. 'What do you want for it?' The man told him. 'Is there anything wrong with it?' 'No.' 'I'll buy it.' They shook hands there and then. The deal was done before they alighted at Dereham Station.

Thus 'Whitehall' passed into the family hands, a fine villa in the Italianate manner, with a tower, ground floor windows reaching almost to the ground, much stained glass, and excellent grounds. Now demolished. In 'Whitehall' H. H. lived with his wife, Elizabeth, and their servants, gardener, dog and cats.

Elizabeth lay abed when I knew her. It was a fashionable thing then to be a permanent invalid. She was placid, and fed visiting small boys on grapes. She died before I was five.

Three sons, as in a fairy tale, were born to H. H. – Nelson, Gordon and Stanley. Stanley arrived on March 12th, 1896. Nelson died of a neglected appendix at his public school, Bishop Stortford, but that didn't stop H. H. despatching his other two sons there.

Stanley, my father, knuckled down under his father, as boys did in those days, and ran the men's outfitting department of the Aldiss shop. His brother ran the furnishing department.

When the First World War thundered across Europe in 1914, my father joined the Royal Flying Corps. He saw action in Egypt, Mesopotamia, and Gallipoli, recorded on stacks of sepia photographs now in my care. When the war was over, he married a young lady from Peterborough, Elizabeth May Wilson, nicknamed Dot. I, their only son, was born on Tuesday, 18th August 1925, in an odd humour.

We lived in a spacious flat over the shop. My first memory is of the decorations on the walls. There were paintings of camels, framed certificates to show that father was twice mentioned in despatches, and a photograph of him looking jovial in pierrot outfit. He had a taste for fun in those days. Nor did he appear to take religion very seriously, despite all his good work for the church. 'Hail, smiling morn,' he would sing when he got up on rainy days. Many hymns were turned laughingly to subversive use.

Father was an athlete. We went to see him swim, run, and hurdle. Once he won a tortoiseshell clock for swimming. He was a handsome man. I admired him greatly. Hero-worshipped him, in fact.

What a paradise for a child was that conglomeration of Aldiss shops. Beyond description. Gormenghast was no more inexhaustible than the property of H. H. Aldiss. There were cottages, where staff had 'lived in' in the old style, now decaying and stuffed with inscrutable objects, brass bedheads wrapped in straw, wicker bathchairs, dummies, wardrobes, the makings of wash-hand-stands, boxes of this, boxes of that. There was a factory, so-called, crammed with carpets and lino and coconut matting, very abrasive to a boy's bare knees. There were dark passages leading to fitting rooms or stores or cabinets full of empty boxes. There were two enormous underground stoke holes, where furnaces were fired which kept the whole organisation heated. There were also stables and attendant outhouses, including tack-rooms, presided over by a ferocious being, enemy of all living things under the age of ten, called Nelson Monument. The horses stomped out from the yard wearing black sables, for H. H. Aldiss also did funerals. The firm would see you safely from the cradle to the grave. In various nooks throughout this rambling territory, one stumbled on little bands of people doing whatever they did. Tailors sitting cross-legged, making up suits. Milliners, presided over by a hostile fat lady, making hats. Dressers, carpenters, removal men, dress-makers. Busy men, idle men with pencils tucked behind their ears, men with pins in their lapels. Each a world in itself, where one was greeted with various degrees of interest, affection, or derision. The perfect playground, until my father or grandfather appeared, wrathful, to larrup you round the legs with a yardstick for interrupting the great Congregationalist God of Work.

Upstairs in the hat department was a young lady with whom I was enchanted. How beautiful she was. I loved her desperately. She sat me on her knee and would tease me unbearably. Yet I endured it because sometimes she would hug and kiss me. The scent and warmth of her were enough to burst my heart with excitement.

In this environment, I thought myself the luckiest of boys. I could run wild. Nobody knew where I went. I used to rove at large beyond the shop, exploring the back alleys of the country town, sometimes being allowed into people's houses. I was always curious to see how others lived. Sometimes I could get our terrier, Gyp, dear faithful Gyp, to come with me; but his absences were noticed more easily than mine.

I was tremendously happy and yet desperately insecure.

My maternal grandparents, the Wilsons, had four children, three sons and then a daughter, who was to marry my father. The sons grew into cheerful men, my uncles Allen, Bert, and Ernest; I loved them all greatly, my Uncle Bert best of all. My mother shared in the family love of fun, but she had in addition a vein of melancholy which went deep and was reinforced by what befell her early in married life.

When we buried my Aunt Dorothy in East Dereham, I

went to the council offices to pay for the gravedigger. I took the opportunity to enquire if there was any record of a daughter being born to my parents and dying soon after birth.

The clerk found nothing in the burial record. Unexpectedly, she wrote to me some months later, to say that she had found the information I required by accident, while looking through the old register of funeral fees. On 17th February 1920 my mother had given birth to a baby girl; since the child was stillborn, it was buried in unconsecrated ground without a funeral. The grave was unmarked. Such was the custom at the time. Thus, in 1984, a ghost was laid which had haunted me for over half a century.

One feature of the story is particularly poignant. When telling us about this dead daughter, my mother always insisted to my sister and me that the baby lived only six weeks, and that she was the prettiest little thing.

The record showed that the child had been born dead. That remission of six weeks remained my mother's consoling fantasy. 'I understood the child was deformed,' Aunt Dorothy said once, with a certain stately relish.

Hardly had I learned to understand speech before I was aware that my arrival in the world profoundly disappointed my mother. She was still mourning the daughter who had died five years earlier. There was no room in her heart for a boy.

'Your sister's with the angels.' Avenging angels, I thought.

Mine was the complete unquestioning love for my mother with which all children are born. But I soon learnt how conditional was her love. If I did anything 'wrong' – which is to say deviated from her instructions through ignorance – she would threaten that she would never love me again.

I lived in terror of this threat. With it went the reinforcing threat that she would run away and leave me.

Sturdy child though I was, such menaces had an intense impact upon me. Every time they were uttered, I suffered a 'bilious attack'. Whether my mother comprehended cause and effect, or cared, I know not. Every attack was dosed with bitter medicine. Then I would recover and disappear into the warrens of the shop. I longed to be dead. Living was too great a pain.

Something else. Even now, the admission comes hard. Mother would threaten me with her imminent death. 'I may be dead tomorrow,' she would say. I would wake in the night in a sweat, wondering if she was still alive, listening for a sound.

It is difficult to reach back to the feelings of that terrorised boy. My one comfort was that, if things got too bad, I could tell my father and he would be on my side, would surely set everything right. I never put it to the test. My much adored father beat me regularly; I never questioned that I deserved what I got. Worse than being beaten was the way he made me shake hands with him afterwards to prove that we were still friends.

Such early experiences are always echoed in fiction, either consciously or unconsciously. It was with considerable interest that I read – many years after the death of my parents – what one perceptive critic, Joseph Milicia, wrote about my novel, *Hothouse*, for the Baen Books edition:

> In an adventure tale without a home-world, the atmosphere of dream may be no less intense; in fact it may be intensified by the disturbing sense that there is no place to wake up to. This is the case in *Hothouse*, where

home is an easily invaded village that must in any case be abandoned after childhood, and also in Aldiss' first novel, *Nonstop (Starship)*, where 'home' itself is a subject for questioning and exploring. In either situation, the comfort of home disappears and the sense of alienation, frighteningly felt as a waking nightmare, permeates the narrative.

It is a perceptive piece of criticism, which needs to be read all through.

Mother would say prayers with me, both of us kneeling, at bedtime. We prayed to our Congregationalist god that her next child would be a little girl. How we prayed! Mother grew larger; she took longer rests after lunch; she wept more. I got whooping cough.

There's the touch that transforms these mean anecdotes into history. Nowadays, whooping cough scarcely exists; in the early thirties, it was still a killer of young children. My attack was serious; I became a stumbling block in the path of the procreational process.

April 1931. The house was quiet. Our maid read a book to me. Doctor Duygan was closeted with mother. A wailing cry arose. Father came to me smiling. 'You have a baby sister.' So was my sister Betty born, in the middle of Chapter Two of *Alice in Wonderland*. I was taken to the bedroom door, where mother lay in bed cradling a red-faced infant in her arms. Then I was rushed from the house without ceremony, golliwog, cough and all.

Not my father but one of the men from the shop drove me the sixty miles to Grandma Wilson's house. There I was dumped.

That period in exile lasted for six weeks; it was my

equivalent of Dickens' spell in the blacking factory. For many years I was far too ashamed to speak of it to anyone, anyone. It was the final confirmation that I was unwanted. The illness increased. Twelve of my milk teeth were removed. My golliwog was burnt when I was sick on it – another silent martyr to the whoop. I was careful not to let my well-meaning grandmother see how deeply I suffered. Once when I ran to the window because I thought I heard the familiar sound of our car horn, she asked me what I was doing. 'I saw a dog I liked,' I lied.

In the story of our century a number of people equivalent to the entire population of the U. S. has died through war, genocide, various ingenious forms of extermination, plague, and famine. This is my trivial testament, the history of this mortal.

Nor have I cared to set my history within any kind of social-historical framework. For those who want such things, let me conjure up the kitchen table in our flat above the H. H. Aldiss shop. It was a table about which I was happy to linger as soon as I could toddle. There my mother worked companionably with our maid, Elizabeth – 'Diddy' to me. (How we wept when Diddy left to be married. Like Grandmother Wilson, she was a farmer's daughter, and I was sometimes allowed to ride in her father's spanking pony-and-trap down the leafy lanes to Gressenhall.)

Mother and Diddy prepared unlimited delicious meals on that table. The rabbit pies, apple pies, buns, cherry cakes, jam roly-polys, and so on would then be transferred to our oven, which was heated by three paraffin burners. The table would then be vigorously scrubbed down. Through usage, the texture of the wooden surface resembled the coat of a polar bear when it first comes heavily out of the water. The two women were always happy and fulfilled when working together, chatting of this and that, about our table.

How often did I think of that scene when exiled at the Peterborough house. There seemed no end to the weeks until I was allowed home again, unprepared for change.

Thus my earliest years. They seem to comprise a complete small life, choked with incident and emotion. I had escaped from my playpen to become a little wild character – a photograph shows me about to indulge in my passion for climbing trees, dressed in an Indian suit, with head-dress – for I never wished to be a cowboy – the cucumber smell of a crushed elder stem still reminds me of those days – whose thought processes had a natural death with the birth of my sister. My second sister, perhaps I should say.

Those early years were transfused with a grief not mine. I call it grief now. Then it was life, since I knew no alternative to it.

Once I saw a steel engraving of an angelic child hovering over a boy walking on a hillside. My dead sister became the steel engraving angel, always hovering, always threatening by her absence.

Why my mother was unable to shake off her obsessive melancholy and accept me for what I was I cannot tell. The Victorian habit of conventional mourning had been burdensome; yet it did provide opportunity for the release of sorrow. After World War I, the custom was abandoned by a younger generation who would hear no more about death. In the face of so many war dead, a black tie was an impertinence.

My grandmother, Elizabeth Wilson, a member of an older generation, went into widow's weeds when my grandfather died in 1926 and never came out of them. I remember her in Peterborough dressed only in black, the dress adorned with black beads and a high white collar tight to the throat: the costume of an earlier age. My mother had no similar custom on which to fall back. One must suppose that my father, being unable to comfort her, being unable adequately to enter into her feelings, introduced a note of estrangement which then became part of their marriage.

Meanwhile, there I was, caught helplessly in that early phase, without reassurance, feeling inadequate at the bottom of a wall of sorrow, not knowing where to turn or where to find comfort.

Yet I was willing to comfort others (the great recourse of the uncomforted). In 1929 my father became so ill of a bronchial complaint that our doctor told him he must spend the winter in South Africa if he wished to live. Mother broke this news to me dolefully in her bedroom, one afternoon after she had been resting.

'Never mind, mummy,' said I, with all the assurance of four years. 'I'll look after you.'

Her response was to turn away and weep, her elbows resting on the chest-of-drawers.

When I came as an adult to study the life of Mary Shelley, I well understood her feelings of isolation caused by the death of her illustrious mother, Mary Wollstonecraft. It would not be emphasising my loss too greatly to say that it was as if I too had lost the comfort of a mother.

The confirmation of that loss was my six week exile in Peterborough.

Nothing was the same when I was restored coughless to my home. The baby was the centre of attention and, two-and-a-bit years later, when I was almost eight, my parents packed me off to boarding school, and at boarding schools I remained for ten years, until I was called up into the army in 1943.

In my second exile, all the family were involved. My grandfather, as I have said, married again, which caused divisions among the relations who could accept the idea of a seventy-year-old man marrying again and those who could not. My father, ever dependent on his father, was in the former class. The shock my grandfather gave everyone was enhanced by his brilliant stroke in marrying the attractive cashier with whom he had enjoyed a relationship for some while.

H. H. and Dorothy had only nine years together before the old boy died. According to the story, retold by my mother, my father begged H. H. on his deathbed to divide the business in two, or else there would be trouble. 'You must fight your own battles from now on, Stanley,' said H. H., and died as he had lived, never the most sympathetic of fathers.

Within a year, father had lost the battle and sold up his share of the business. We could not stay in East Dereham. What a disgrace! An Aldiss lopped off from the Aldiss business! The Congregational Church gave father a memorial Bible, suitably inscribed, as we disappeared to settle into a terrace house in Gorleston-on-Sea. I say 'we'; how it happened as far as I was concerned was that I left Dereham as usual at the onset of a new school term, and returned to a small house by the sea. Friends and familiar things gone. Nothing in my life seemed secure. This was in 1938 when war also was on its way.

My one friend was my sister. Contrary to the doctrinal pronouncements of Dr Freud and Dr Spock, I loved my sister greatly; we were as close as we could be considering the five-year gap in our ages. Betty was terribly bright and funny, and more rebellious than I. We had a wonderful time together at Gorleston, and used to walk barefoot from our house to the promenade and back, where we would spend all day. The Punch-and-Judy routines we had by heart, being proficient at all the comic voices. In the winter, huge waves provided a spectacle, breaking against the old Dutch pier which marked the mouth of the River Yare.

My father was at a complete loss without the shop and his cheerful assistants. I was secretly relieved by that loss. Even at twelve, I knew I had no interest whatever in outfitting, in measuring people, or indeed in clothes. I also knew that I would have obeyed my father's wishes like a dutiful son and have 'gone into the business' had we stayed in Dereham.

By then I had developed what were to be lifelong interests. My prep school was a Dotheboys establishment whose educational structure was founded on punishment, boredom, and semi-starvation; there I learned to enjoy the mercy of reading, and began myself to make books. To quell my homesickness – worst at night – I smuggled in a small kaleidoscope, which I viewed under the bedclothes with the aid of a torch; the tumbling patterns delighted me and encouraged a feeling for aesthetics. I was also allowed a microscope and a telescope, since those were not toys. (Still to need toys at eight!) From those instruments grew an interest in science, and the hidden world.

Before the war came – an event prayed against with fervour and no effect – my father put some black boot polish on his sideburns to hide encroaching greyness (he would then have been forty-three) and volunteered for the R.A.F. They turned him down as too old. This was a cruel blow. From then on, he became increasingly bitter.

He sold the house in Gorleston and took us to live in Devon – almost a foreign country to us. We could hardly understand the local accent. I was put into a public school on the fringes of Exmoor, West Buckland School. After some casting around, my father bought a poor little business outside Barnstaple, a combined general store and sub-post office. There he worked day and night without complaint, and mother worked beside him. She liked a laugh and company, and had a jollier time than he did. By this time, her melancholy had dispersed, and Betty and I were on good terms with her. We did a lot of laughing and singing.

One of our treats was to go to the cinema. Attached to our outside fence was a billboard on which the Regal, Barnstaple, advertised. As payment for this slot, the cinema allowed us two free tickets each week. Betty and I went to the cinema just as often as we could manage.

This was the phase in life when Betty was crazy about Roy Rogers. We sat through innumerable Republic Pictures starring that singing cowboy, with Trigger, his white horse, and featuring old George Gabby Hayes and the Sons of the Pioneers. My tastes ran more towards 'thrillers', in particular those thrillers featuring Humphrey Bogart or Edward G. Robinson. I was mad about Eddie G., and wrote to him in Hollywood for a signed photograph, which duly arrived from Warner Brothers. I still have it.

Another Warner Brothers star was Ida Lupino, the beautiful loser. For me, she generated more emotional current than Betty Grable – but rather less than the sumptuous Hedy Lamarr. Hedy was not merely gorgeous, she was foreign and had appeared on the screen in the nude, thus adding greatly to her attraction.

My reading tastes were slightly more sophisticated than my film tastes. Anxiety had converted me to insomnia at an early age – at least by nine – and this enabled me to devour many books during the hours of night. By the time we were expelled from East Dereham, that poisoned Eden, I had read a wide variety of novels, including *Jane Eyre*, *Wuthering Heights*, *John Halifax, Gentleman* (which I loathed for its false piety), some Dickens, several novels by Zola, and Murger's *Vie de Boheme*, which gave me a longing for the bohemian life never entirely assuaged or forgotten.

I was also reading all kinds of ephemeral rubbish with avidity. A friend called Harold Leeds started me on 'The Schoolboy's Own Library', by giving me several of the fourpenny volumes he had finished with. So I met the lads of St Jim's, the lads of Rookwood, and the lads of Greyfriars, those three great fictitious English public schools which, I suppose, most boys of my generation and before encountered. All were the invention of Frank Richards, a most prolific author who used different pen names for the different schools. I much preferred St Jim's, with Tom Merry and Co., but somehow it was the boring Billy Bunter and Greyfriars which survived in the public mind. The adventures of these lively characters appeared in two weekly magazines, *The Magnet* and *The Gem*, which flourished between the two world wars and embodied, rather like P. G. Wodehouse stories, a sort of sporting Edwardian view of the world, with stern codes of conduct cheek-by-jowl with horseplay. *The Gem* was my weekly reading for many years, although I was forbidden to read it at my loony prep school, on the grounds that it was subversive.

Eventually *Modern Boy* overtook *The Gem* in my affections. To *Modern Boy* I owe a happy debt. It was full of the future and of exciting technical developments, like the building of the Channel Tunnel. It carried stories of all kinds of sports, including motor-racing. Sir Malcolm Campbell occasionally wrote for *Modern Boy*. So did Captain W. E. Johns, whose stories about Biggles, the flying ace, first appeared in those illustrious pages in serial form. So did Murray Roberts, whose hero – and mine – was Captain Justice.

Captain Justice was a great original as far as I was concerned. He was a tall man with a pointed beard who smoked cigars and wore elegant white ducks. He sorted out any menaces to civilisation which were too big for Britain and America to handle. Justice lived with his entourage on Station A in mid-Atlantic. Station A had a mighty mast, to the top of which was moored the 'Flying Cloud', Justice's famous airship, capable of turning invisible at the touch of a switch. This innovation was the work of the scientist of Justice's party, Professor Flaznagel. Who could ever forget those characters, the genial Doctor O'Malley, Len Connor, or the irrepressible Midge?

Justice fought off menaces from the Sargasso, an interstellar gas which plunged the world into darkness, a hellish telepathic dictatorship arising in Africa, a runaway planet, gigantic robots, and many other science-fictional phenomena. It was all meat and drink in the pre-teens.

Out of sentiment, I still possess some of Captain Justice's adventures. They are totally unreadable now, alas. All cliché. The irrepressible Midge should have been repressed long ago.

The war did for *Modern Boy*. But by then I had discovered the science fiction magazines. A curious coincidence reinforced my early addiction.

When Britain declared war on Nazi Germany, in September 1939, the Aldiss family was in a caravan on a wild stretch of the North Cornish coast near Tintagel. We stood looking blankly at the peaceful Atlantic as the news came over the radio. My father went to an estate agent and bought a nearby bungalow, then standing deserted on the cliffs.

We drove to inspect it. A warm autumn sun shone in on the bare interior, on the naked floorboards. The bungalow was spotlessly clean, entirely empty. Except that on the window seat lay a copy of *Fantasy*, a British sf magazine. It was mine immediately.

The lead story was by John Russell Fearn. The cover depicted a scene in Picadilly Circus, where gigantic caterpillars were busy overturning double-decker buses. The fire brigade had been called out. The firemen were spraying the crawling menaces with quick-drying plaster of Paris. Within a year of publication, those fire brigades were in reality called out on more serious business.

We used to sit in the front room of that bungalow looking out at the great sun as it sank into the bronze Atlantic. It was a season of stillness, of ominously calm weather. Sometimes a convoy would be outlined against the setting sun. We listened to the news. My father did not speak.

Similar calm prevailed in May 1940, when France fell, and Britain fought on alone. My father then took the smaller of his two shot-guns from a corner and handed it to me; we expected to use them in earnest within a month or two.

By that period, we had moved into the house behind the general store. It was still possible to find science fiction here and there. In particular I had come across *Astounding* magazine and the works of H. G. Wells. Wells was my preference: three of his stories in particular caught my imagination, *The Time Machine*, imperishably one of the brilliant books associated with science fiction, 'The Country of the Blind', and 'The Door in the Wall', which I read over and over again, relishing its poignance, in which I felt something of my own situation. A door had closed for ever.

What I liked about *Astounding* was its sense of continuance, and the subjects under discussion, though in some mysterious way they lacked the metaphorical quality which is such an enrichment in Wells's best writing.

The correspondence columns of *Astounding* in the late thirties bandied about the name of Nietzsche in connection with the rejection of religion and the concept of a superman. I had no particular affection for supermen, but Nietzsche sounded interesting. None of his books could be found in Barnstaple. A friend recommended I join the local Atheneum, which had a good library. What this solemn club thought when a thirteen year old tried to enlist I have no idea; however, they allowed me to join, and there I sat in one of their stiff leather armchairs, reading *Thus Spake Zarathustra*. To my great benefit and confusion.

Thus developed a taste for exotic foreign names. In the Atheneum, I discovered Chinese poetry through Arthur Waley's translations. At school, I stumbled over Ouspensky, whom I was later to send up in *Barefoot in the Head*. A top grade lunatic.

Meanwhile, I wrote. At home, at school, I wrote.

West Buckland was a rough tough school. The freedom of wild Exmoor was much to be enjoyed. We even swam in some of the pools and corries up there, the water being crystal clear but freezing. When we were old enough to join the Home Guard, we were able to get into the little pubs at Stagshead and Brayford and become drunk on beer or cider.

Before leaving those prison years behind, I should say something about the twisted intellectual development which led to my becoming a writer. I believe that that ambition formed within me when I was eight or nine, although it may be hindsight which suggests this.

Certainly I was interested in writing at an early age. The study of Latin improved this faculty. I did nine years of Latin and became proficient enough almost to enjoy the language.

I also enjoyed English Grammar, a subject no longer taught in British schools, which seems a sad deficiency. It is much more important for a writer to know the intricacies of the hard geological backbone of his medium than to understand how to operate a computer efficiently. The death or permanent displacement of the apostrophe is imminent.

As well as being interested in writing, I was interested in story-telling – the two things are separate. Story-telling became almost a source of salvation, certainly a source of pride when I had little to be proud of, at an early age.

The first public school to which I was sent (before West Buckland) was Framlingham College in Suffolk, a thriving hothouse for bullies, toadies, and all creeping things. There my shyness and a propensity for making weird gadgets (especially light planes, board games, and cardboard things which jumped out of lockers) led to my being called The Professor. I acquired greater fame as a story-teller.

The Junior Dormitory was a horrendous place in which some twenty beds were ranged round the walls under the long windows. Each bed had a locker beside it. There was no other furniture, no carpet or rug on the bare floor, no flicker of a curtain. Picture a workhouse in Dickens's time. Thus were young English gentlemen brought up.

At Lights Out, the rule was strictly No Talking. Nevertheless, a subversive tradition survived of telling tales. The wretched inmates had no campfires, but their thirst for narrative remained intact. At the start of a new term, each infant in turn had to sit in the dark and tell a story. It was an ordeal. Most stories were greeted with derision. The most derided boys were silenced, often rather forcibly. The survivors lived to spout again. Gradually champions emerged. The two champions in my time were B. B. Gingell and I.

Gingell was a skilled and witty teller. His handicap was his subject-matter, which generally centred round some contemptible denizen of the animal kingdom, an otter (I think he once purveyed Henry Williamson's classic over the course of a spring term), a beaver, a deer, a wolf, or even a snake. Whereas I went for planets, wonders of the future, and the re-hashed adventures of Captain Justice. What's more, I did all the voices.

I would be in full blood-freezing spate when the door of the dormitory would be flung open. In would stride the housemaster, Mr Broughton, 'Bonzo', in his gown. 'Who's talking?' My hand would rise into the air with memorable sloth. I would then be made to bend over and be given Six with the cane on my pyjamas. Six was particularly painful when the previous Six had not yet healed.

Such was my first reward for my art. After which, the astringent remarks of critics could hardly be expected to compare in cutting power. I have often wondered how many other science fiction writers had such a formidable christening in the line of duty. Very few.

The beatings in no way deflected my purpose. At the much pleasanter West Buckland, there was no oral tradition. I wrote my stories down.

It proved a better way to fame. The stories were pungently primed with sex and violence and general schoolboy naughtiness. Each carried a little tempter or blurb under its title, in the manner of *Weird* and *Astounding* and other pulps I was reading at the time. Innuendo was rampant. I remember only two tempters, on stories whose names I have forgotten. One concerned a newspaper man who died in suspiciously lubricious circumstances: 'The editor's incision was final.' There was one about some Chicago vice racketeers: 'They went to New York for a change of obscenery.'

These stories were hired out at a hypothetical penny a time. They changed hands rapidly. The danger with them was that they might fall into the hands of authority; I would then have been beaten and expelled.

The Sixth Form at West Buckland was a good one. We were a tight-knit community who had survived the arduous ascent through the school. A lot of wit and laughter enlivened our days. Without the moral support of my friends, I doubt if I would have had the nerve to keep producing.

The headmaster was not above conducting a desk-to-desk search. One of the worst features of the public school system was the lack of privacy; the unscrupulous were set over us to teach us scruples.

At the end of each term, we held a solemn ceremony. My stories were sealed into a large Huntley & Palmer biscuit tin, which my friend Bowler and I then took and buried in a rabbit hole in a nearby wood, to await resurrection next term. Shortly afterwards, a new wave of myxamatosis swept England.

In my last term at West Buckland, I wrote and acted in our house concert. I co-directed with our housemaster, Harold Boyer, who has been a staunch friend ever since. Home was twelve miles from school, yet my parents did not attend my night of glory. Well, it was wartime.

But it was a relief to escape into the relative safety and comfort of the army. No military training came hard after public school.

All these years, I suffered the incommunicable pain of rejection. I read deeply in psychology and philosophy to try and heal myself. Later, mother would laugh to recall how, when she was out walking with us, I would pretend to fall down dead; she never comprehended that I was really longing to be dead; the distress signal did not get through. But how could she guess, for at other times Betty and I, when in manic mood, would straggle beside her in the street, pretending to be hunchbacks, cripples, or imbeciles? Then she would shriek with laughter and say, 'Oh, you're not with me, you're nothing to do with me, nobody will think I have idiot children like that.'

The army proved a great healer, particularly when I was sent on a troopship to India, into a third exile. I forgot about my family situation and enjoyed the independence. To be abroad was wonderful – Betty and I had always longed to go abroad. How delighted we had been when a relation wrote to say that Grandma Wilson's maiden name, Ream, was explained by the fact that she came of Huguenot stock fleeing from Rheims. So we had a pint or two of French blood in us to alleviate the boring English stuff.

Anything exotic we loved. India and Burma were nothing if not exotic.

Life in the ranks of the British Army in the East in wartime was extremely hard. Full of laughs, of course. The redeeming feature was that most of it was conducted outside, in the sun, the glorious sun. I never forget the beauty of some of the places we visited. Of my experiences in India and Burma, I wrote a novel, *A Soldier Erect*, because I wanted people to see how things were. As far as I know, nobody else who served in the ranks ever spoke out on that subject.

The war provided an initiation rite for young men. If you came through it intact, it gave you a sense of privilege. It made you – and of course in many ways it unmade you.

Even when riven by war, Burma was intensely seductive, a country of magic. Late in 1944, our division, the Second British Division, moved into action from the area of Kohima and rolled south, crossing the Manipur River into the Letha Range. As I reported in my novel, our commander addressed us before we went into action, finishing by quoting the famous speech Shakespeare gives to Henry V before Agincourt:

And gentlemen in England now abed
Shall think themselves accursed they were not here
And hold their manhoods cheap whiles any speaks
That fought with us upon St Crispin's Day.

We were caught up in an enterprise which united us all, in which we could accept that an individual's life was of less importance than the survival and ultimate victory of his tribe. Our hardships – the fact that we saw no water at all for six weeks, for instance – were a source of pride. It is sad that human beings rarely achieve such unity in time of peace. We called ourselves the Fourteenth Army, 'The Forgotten Army'; so it was, and so it has remained ever since. There was almost no media coverage, as we would say nowadays; Assam and Burma were simply too difficult to get to, and all transport was stretched to its limits and beyond. Nor were there poets to speak for us, in the way that Sassoon and Wilfred Owen and many other tongues spoke for the war of the trenches. There was Alun Lewis, it is true, but his was a minor voice – and he shot himself before going into action. Nor have any novels come out of that campaign to my knowledge, except my own.

Before moving from Yazagyo to Kalewa, where we established a bridgehead on the River Chindwin, we crossed the Tropic of Cancer and, once over the Chindwin, were on the dry flat plains which lead to Mandalay, killing Japanese all the way. Soon Mandalay was again in British hands.

One of the awful features of being in action was the fear that you might be killed before you had really enjoyed a woman. It made dying terrible. I was no virgin; nor had I really experienced an intense affair. But even small children experience rending sexual passion, as I did for the girl in the hat department. In kindergarten, we were very wanton. When I once innocently came home, aged five, and told my mother how we played Cows and Milkmaids, with the boys being the cows, she phoned the school in a panic so great that it was a wonder that she did not ring the police and the Milk Marketing Board as well.

Three of the girls at that school I adored and felt, and got them to feel me. Sheila, Heather, and Margaret. I proposed marriage to Margaret at the age of six, and she consented – another family joke! – but it was Heather and her beauty which captivated me. Heather had her tonsils out at the age of eight and became fat. My passion faltered.

Later, I was fortunate in having an affair with an older woman; all that Colette has to say on that subject is correct. In Norwich, during the war, it was possible to have knee-tremblers with school-girls after dark for half-a-crown. But what one dreamed of in Burma was a real grown-up no-holds-barred intimate affair. In India there were only whores available to other ranks. Some of the whores were extremely beautiful, especially the Chinese ones in Calcutta.

My temptation here is to run on about Burma, as it is to remain silent about the more personal side of my life. Burma was and – as I understand from my elder daughter who has just visited it – remains a magical country. As for the magical country of sexuality, my parents teased me so much whenever I had a girl friend, no doubt because of their own underlying sexual malaise, that I would go to any lengths to cover my tracks. Cunning and deflection I used to remove their attention. This habit persisted into the army. I confided in no one. My affairs were my affair. On the whole, this seems a good rule in life. On one occasion when I tried to live more openly, much misery resulted.

After Burma, with its decaying piles of Japanese bodies and its immense moons, back to India – or rather to Chittagong, now in Bangladesh. In Chittagong, we were so delighted to see water again after the Burmese dry season that we swam in the river there – practically an open sewer – and came to no harm. We were fit, hard, long-haired, lean, randy.

The Fourteenth Army, that raggle-taggle army of many races and tongues, was breaking up. I was posted on detachment to Bombay, to work a radio link connecting up various units then preparing as a task force to invade Singapore by sea, code name Operation Zipper. I lived in a rather grand private house near Breach Kandy, where I swam most days, and began to know and like Indians a little better.

Then to a purgatory sixty miles outside Bangalore, to a vicious bit of jungle to practise more jungle warfare. The monsoon was coming. We lived in straw bashas. Under every stone lurked enormous centipedes. Scorpions scuttled everywhere, ants of all dimensions abounded, frogs made the evening intolerable with their boastful cries. Snakes emerged from every bush. Little snakes worked their way down from overhanging trees and through the thatched roof, to fall on top of one's mosquito net; bigger ones slid through the doorways. We killed a monster cobra in the generator room. It was a horrible place. We were there when the atom bombs were dropped on Hiroshima and Nagasaki.

My friend Ted Monks came over to me and said, 'You know those bombs, Brian? They're the things they've been talking about in your science fiction magazines.'

The universe had shifted. What had been alarming fantasy had become reality. We rejoiced. It meant that we were not going to have to invade Singapore by sea, using leaky old landing craft left over from the Mediterranean theatre of war. The A-bomb, in bringing the war to a rapid conclusion, spared many lives.

As the years pass since that time, the dropping of those first atomic bombs – as we used to call nuclear weapons – is increasingly seen as a turning point in human history. So it is worth even a humble witness giving evidence on the matter.

Early in 1945, the Japanese war machine was showing no signs of yielding to intimations of defeat. The American Chiefs of Staff were planning two major operations for launch when the war against Hitler in Europe was over. In November 1945, there was to be Operation Olympic, involving 750,000 men; and in March 1946, Operation Coronet, involving an amazing 1.8 million men, landing in the Tokyo area. At the same time, the U.S. Air Forces were bombing the Japanese islands. On the night of March 9th alone, a raid on Tokyo killed 84,000 people and rendered a million homeless.

In my own forgotten theatre of war, Supremo Mountbatten's forces were being mustered for the dire Operation Zipper, to take place in September 1945. Between Penang and Singapore (all along the Malayan coastline, that is), 182,000 men were to be launched in seaborne landings. The Japanese at this time had over half a million troops in S.E. Asia.

In all these operations, which ran to a scale hitherto unknown, casualties would have been extremely high on both sides. It was clear that the Japanese under pressure would have killed – by gas or shooting or whatever means convenient – all the Allied and Chinese prisoners in their hands. No mercy would have been shown.

No one at the time doubted the evil of the Japanese regime. The Japanese themselves were regarded as both sub-human and superhuman. They seemed to respond to no moral code. Only the dropping of the two bombs could have ended protracted misery – not to the Allies alone, but to the indigenous populations of the Pacific area and S.E. Asia who had the ill fortune to fall under the Japanese yoke. Some 300,000 deaths can be attributed to the bombs on Hiroshima and Nagasaki. It was a small price to pay for the abrupt cessation of that barbarous war.

The Japanese surrender was greeted with universal joy.

The British had come through six years of war. Their country had been broken economically and shattered physically. Moreover, the British troops sent to the East were never given a date for the expiry of their service abroad; it was not like the war in Vietnam, where terms of service were brief; we were out there for keeps, as far as we knew.

After the surrender, there was another messy job to be done. The Japanese invaders had somehow to be shovelled back into their homelands. That was the next item awaiting the victors.

I was posted to an Indian barracks in simmering Madras, and there became a member of the Twenty-Sixth Indian Division. We sailed eastwards, across the equator, to Padang in Sumatra, where our task was to disarm a Japanese army and send the invaders packing back to their distant homeland. More adventures!

During my year in Sumatra, my job was at first to work a radio set which kept us in touch with ALFSEA, our higher command. We operated to Singapore, to Hong Kong, and back to Delhi, as well as to local detachments around Sumatra and posts in Malaya such as Port Swettenham. Meanwhile, I was forcing myself to face a more personal communication problem.

All the time I was abroad, I kept a diary, although this was strictly forbidden on active service, in case it fell into the hands of the enemy. I also wrote a few short stories. At school, as I have said, I had been a prolific and popular writer of short stories – science fiction, crime, pornography, and conventional. These themes often blended. Forty years after leaving West Buckland, I met a rather distinguished man who had prevailed upon his parents to remove him from the school, on the grounds of its sheer awfulness, cold, discomfort, and general misery. To my surprise, he remembered me as someone who had been kind and comforted him, and had lent him my long story – which he still remembered – about the adventures of a penny. My first audience was grateful to me, many years after the event!

The determination grew in me while in Sumatra to write as truthful an account as possible of life in the East. I felt that the British were blind to its beauties. The evidence for this blindness was all around me; while I loved Sumatra, my army friends longed only to be home. They felt their lives were in a state of suspension, whereas mine was in full spate. The exotic was a state of fulfilment.

With some manoeuvring, I got myself in charge of the camp theatre, where we had shows, films, and dances. I became the unit draughtsman, and redecorated the theatre with paintings and caricatures. This gave me more leisure to write, edit a magazine, and generally enjoy tropical existence.

The eventual return to England marked my fourth exile. I had no particular wish to get back. When I returned, the England I had known as a child had gone. A new harsh grey post-war world established itself in which I found myself considerably at a loss. I could not even comprehend the monetary system, and confused florins and half-crowns. The behaviour of people was mysterious. The towns were filthy, with evidence of bomb damage everywhere, while rationing for some years became more stringent than it had been during the war. It was cold. The sun never reached zenith. Women were prudish and cautious. Another generation was coming along, rancid young Teds with something ugly to prove because they had missed the action.

The war aged people. It was not until the 1960s that a law was passed permitting everyone to be young.

My chances of entering a 'good' job were two: taking over my father's business – an option already shot from under me – or entering my Uncle Bert's architectural firm. Architecture had been with me since birth. Uncle Bert had designed the new front for H. H. Aldiss in East Dereham (and there it still stands, although the premises behind have been sold off for some awful new development), and done much work round about Peterborough. He would be happy to take me into the firm, along with my cousin John.

Already I was several leagues behind in the rat race. The thought of another seven years study, punctuated by exams, which an architectural degree requires, was too much for me. And I knew I had to master the art of writing.

My father had sold his general store, and was acting as manager in a gents' outfitter in Barnstaple, in Devon. I was as indifferent to that trade as ever. During my demobilisation leave, I took a train up to Oxford and got a job in a bookshop. I told the bookseller that I was ready to set to work that day – which I did, later finding myself a room round the corner from the shop.

Oxford's a charming city – not free of blemishes, but its blemishes can become dear. I soon found friends, and began to enjoy life. My parents decided, rather to my surprise, to join me and buy a house in Oxford. Which was good for Betty, who went to the local Art School. For me, the advantages were less obvious; I had to go back under the parental roof. I had a girl friend, a delightful mixture of effrontery and shyness, of whom I used to see a lot. Often it was one or two in the morning before I got home. My father disapproved of such behaviour. One night

I returned to find him in pyjamas and dressing-gown, awaiting me in the kitchen.

I had been the most submissive of sons, hoping always to please him. This was too much. After glowering at him, I asked him what he thought he was doing. He weakened, and said he thought he'd stay up to make me some hot chocolate.

'I don't want it,' I said, and went to bed. No more was said.

It took me eight years before I had gained enough skill and confidence to leave the bookshop behind, to be independent as a writer. By then, two books had been published, *The Brightfount Diaries*, a light-hearted account of work in a fictitious bookshop, and *Space, Time, and Nathaniel*, a collection of stories in the sf vein.

It might appear that I have so far painted a rather negative portrait of my mother. When my sister and I were older, she was supportive, and entered into all we did with enthusiasm. No one was more pleased than she when I began to make a success with writing. In a letter to me from London in 1957, where she went to live after father died, she wrote:

Where to start? Post came half an hour ago as Betty was hurrying to get off – and with it your parcel; she had no time to look at S.T.A.N. or the photographs and I just read bits of your letter to her as she had to hurry away. Now I have got my breath back from all the excitement, just must leave what I have to do and sit down to write. First, many many thanks for all the above-mentioned items. I shall read every word of the book, have already read the Introduction, which I think awfully good. I love the plain bold and eye-catching dust cover; *all success* with it. Perhaps you would kindly send an 'Oxford Mail' when the review is in? . . .

I have just been thinking how my great ambition was to publish a successful book, but am certain that could never have been as much of a thrill as my son doing so. God bless you, and all power to your pen.

I can't go from the subject of your writing without mentioning your dedication in S.T.A.N. I thank you most sincerely for that, and can't tell you how touched I was (and shed a few tears over it) and longed for your dear Father to see it; almost (but not quite) made me feel I ought to stay at '548' . . .

If this letter is more incoherent than usual, it is because I am really excited.

Just as one is hardly a real driver immediately one has passed the driving test – many miles of experience are still needed – it was several years before I felt able to call myself a writer. Or, for that matter, before I felt irrevocably a writer.

Yet I was always irrevocably a writer. The pressure to express something within me was the more intense for the emotional struggles through which I had to fight. I have written of sorrow; yet there were always within me moments of intense joy, just as beneath my conformity was a tough vein of wildness.

Even as a child, the rapid flow of reflections through my mind delighted me. Terror was there, but pleasure and astonishment also, and laughter. I still chuckle aloud at some surprising juxtaposition of thoughts, arriving unheralded. This is the creative vein, unfakeable.

Anything in nature – a bare twig against the sky – can

lighten my mood. When in the army, I came on a metaphor for mind as I swam in the Irrawaddy near Mandalay. That great stream contains veins of icy and of warm water, veins intertwined but never mixing. A swimmer across the river cannot anticipate whether he is about to enter a stream originating from a local tributary or one coursing down from remote sources in the Himalayas. Yet all waters contribute equally to the life of the river, all will finally flood into the distant sea.

Much has been said about the art of writing; it is an inexhaustible subject. The written word, rather than the flint spear, has brought us such civilization as we now enjoy. It is the duty of the writer to fumble his way towards truth. The view, often expressed, that writers are paid liars, holds no appeal for me. At the same time, truth is elusive; if the future is fluid, so is the past, open – like the rest of the universe – to our interpretation of it. Were I to write this article in a year's time, or had I written it a year ago, no doubt the emphases would be different, and those in turn interpreted differently by the reader: there is an art of reading too.

Rejection slips never came my way at first. My early publishers, Faber & Faber, an illustrious imprint, approached me for my first book. I was happy with them for a long time before moving to my present publishers, Jonathan Cape (with a little help from Weidenfeld & Nicolson). Fabers were always extremely civil. My publisher was that most genial and kindly of men, Charles Monteith. And when one went into their old terracotta buildings in Russell Square, one could encounter T. S. Eliot on the stairs and exchange a few words with him. There also I met other Faber authors, including William Golding, a great science fiction reader and future recipient of the Nobel Prize for literature. One is known by the company one keeps, and the company at Fabers helped shape me.

However, it is also necessary to shape oneself. We are many people in our time. When I came across the portrait of Philip Quarles in Aldous Huxley's *Point Counterpoint*, I believed myself to be like that amorphous creature (in fact Huxley intended a portrait of John Middleton Murray). What creature was I really? If godless, why so god-haunted?

All my old inferiorities crowded in again once I was back in England. Eager though I was to see myself published again, to reinforce a budding reputation, I took the time to look at myself in the mirror of my typewriter and write an autobiography, *Twenty to Thirty*. There I anatomised all my qualities. I was disappointed by what I discovered. So much potential, so little achievement! 'By their fruits ye shall know them' seemed to me the bitterest apothegm in the Bible. I had borne no fruit, though I felt myself a great tree. Handicapped by my poor opinion of myself, I had yet to offer the world the diversity within me.

Once I had the picture clear, I proceeded to remould myself. To be a writer is a proud thing, but to be a real writer one must offer up oneself, give out one's own tidings, stand in, as it were, for the figure of wisdom missing in one's own early years. Novels are messages, not only to the reader, but to the self.

Whatever emotional problems I suffered from – as do all young people, I imagine – I never had existential problems. Amorphous I might be – and that was the sort of question to be traded with girl friends in discussions that went on for all hours – but behind it all I was never plagued with doubts about the reality of the world, or of myself planted firmly in the world. Perhaps this was because, through thick or thin, a sense of mission was present in me. Part of the eagerness to write was the eagerness to share experience and reflection.

Introspection was a deeply ingrained habit at this time. I channelled it into the typewriter with energy and excitement, with rejoicing. But being a full-time writer, having no place of work to go but the front bedroom upstairs where I wrote, brought fresh challenges.

It broke up my marriage. I had married in 1948. By 1958, my wife and I had nothing much to say to each other, and only boredom to communicate. Through our lean years, on a miserable salary, dumped out in Kidlington, Oxford's shunned car-worker dormitory suburb, we had stuck together; she had slaved to keep the home going, to earn and save every penny. It was terrible that when life became easier, when some success came my way, she could only shrink from it. She did not respond as I did to the new currents in the arts of the times, to the plays of John Osborne or the novels of the early Amis, to *Waiting for Godot* which brought some spark to that chilly epoch. If I said that she refused to distinguish between John Osborne and John Wyndham, it would seem as if I claimed our poor little marriage died of literary malaise; yet in a way it was so.

What I could not stand was the silences. After a decade of trying to make things work, we began to come apart – no easy matter in those days. Yet how could I say the marriage was a failure, since from it were born my first and deeply cherished children, Clive and Wendy?

To be away from them was another exile. I lacerated myself, as I saw myself deserting them as I had once been deserted. That echo from the past came back, as fresh as ever, reinforced. I could not allow myself to let the pain go. All divorced parents must feel something of that remorse: each must suffer it alone. My writing abilities departed from me, to return only when I dressed the pain of the event in literary form, in the novel about a world where there are no children, *Greybeard*, which is dedicated to Clive and Wendy.

My father died during this period. A large number of marriages disintegrate after the death of a parent. My poor father suffered many heart attacks before giving in. He lived his last two years confined to house and garden, nursed devotedly by my mother, surviving attack after attack. The attacks were terrifying. Then he would recover to potter about the garden, which he kept fanatically neat. Every last twig on hedge and rose was trimmed. He liked to have small bonfires. Once he kept a tiny little fire going for two weeks, sheltering it under a bucket when rain fell. Every morning he would go and look at it, watching the thin spiral of smoke rise up.

He died on the first of June, 1956, on my mother's birthday, with a bunch of his roses by his bedside, and the evening sunlight filtering through the curtains. As his features relaxed in death, he began to look more and more like the Stanley Aldiss of old, the man who had been photographed in a pierrot suit, laughing and making others laugh.

At least he saw and held on his knee the first of my children.

Later, father appeared to me in a dream or vision, standing at the bottom of the stairs which led to the attic room where I slept. He half-raised a fist. His features were distorted in fury. Poor father. He was disappointed and long-suffering.

Such thoughts and more came back to mind as I stood

by Aunt Dorothy's coffin in the town where I was born. My second wife, my children, my sister and her husband also stood there. The pain of the old drama was dead. So were all its actors, except for my sister and me.

Many people are afflicted by a sense of unreality in their lives. They see the years pass by and feel that no meaning has touched them. Perhaps this holds true in all Western societies, as well as those societies which have, for want of better, taken up with Western models. Plato would have no actors in his republic, in case pretence devoured what was real. Plato's fears have proved well-grounded. Actors, despised, almost outcast, until last century, have become something more than respectable. They, together with all those imitation actors, pop stars, TV celebrities, people who are famous for being famous, now receive adulation. They are the millionaires, the courtesans of our system. Solzhenitsyn, escaping to a West he had once admired, snarled at the meretricious falsity of what he found. We have built illusions round us and see no way out of the glass forest.

Much science fiction reflects this dilemma. So does much of my writing; and only in the last volume of the Helliconia trilogy did I dare to lift my head and suggest a possible way out, a way to feel part of the natural world from which 'the ascent of man' has alienated us.

Our family was caught in the glass forest for many years. We could see each other through the trees, but could not touch each other. Only when my father died were we able to perceive how little we knew him – and how desperately he had preserved an isolation he mourned.

The women's lib movement of recent years has shown up the unnecessary poverty of women's lives. Already far-sighted women have looked deeper and seen how men, fathers and families too often suffered from a loneliness in which emotion had withered. My Aunt Dorothy was different from us; within her was something that never withered.

If we can see our difficulties, there is a way of resolving them, or the hope of a way.

Here is what I wrote about sf. If it has a familiar ring, my publishers liked it well enough to make it into a postcard for publicity purposes. 'I love sf for its surrealist verve, its loony non-reality, its piercing truths, its wit, its masked melancholy, its nose for damnation, its bunkum, its contempt for home comforts, its slewed astronomy, its xenophilia, its hip, its classlessness, its mysterious machines, its gaudy backdrops, its tragic insecurity.'

Science fiction has always seemed to me such a polyglot, an exotic mistress, a parasite, a kind of new language coined for the purpose of giving tongue to the demented twentieth century. I have noted an instance already of how it spoke of one decisive event of our century. Another of science fiction's most powerful themes found expression in the fifties and early sixties, the theme of the alien creature that can assume human form and move among human communities undetected, while it works their destruction. No doubt this hideous idea derived from fears in the society at large. It is a cold war theme, and shows how effectively sf can hold a mirror up to our fears and aspirations.

Another popular sf theme was that of the world dictator, the iron man, who rules the globe or the galaxy. When Stalin died in 1953, the world seemed to begin to breathe again, like a corpse reviving among ice fields. Yet another tyranny was over. Slowly the deleterious effects of human misery caused by the Second World War began to drain away, in East and West. Broken places, broken lives, became less obvious. But we still live under the ruination caused by two world wars. The effects of these wars on most European countries, from England in the West to the Ukraine and Russia in the East, cannot be discounted, while, in the Far East, the cicatrices of those upheavals are no less apparent.

Sf was my mode of expression. My worlds became watertight compartments, like my own life-experience. A new compartment opened when the death of my marriage caused me to lose my home and go to live alone in a run-down district of Oxford.

I rented one room in Paradise Square, soon to fall under the bulldozers. A multi-storey car park now stands where I lived for three years, at No. 12. I had a papier-maché suitcase containing my possessions. My wife had custody of the typewriter. In Woolworths I bought a knife, fork and spoon. No. 12 housed in its crumbling rooms one or two eccentric undergraduates, together with one or two reporters or subeditors from the local paper, *The Oxford Mail*, of which I was then Literary Editor.

We had an alcoholic among us, Len Aitken, whose avowed intention was to drink himself to death. Len was excellent company and used to sell gags to comedians like Ken Dodd for half-a-crown a time. There is nothing like an alcoholic around to make things hum. For a while I became somewhat like the wild boy who had once run about East Dereham after dark.

No. 12 was owned by George and Penny Halcrow, Penny being the daughter of Edgar Wallace. George was the kindest of landlords. I was supposed to pay seven-and-sixpence a week for the room, but George knew how broke I was and often let me off. The house had been occupied by the Indians and Chinese who worked in his Indian and Chinese restaurants. They had walked out – so the story went – because they couldn't stand the conditions. Well, it was a bit squalid. The loo, which was outside, was damp, and great black slugs like animated turds crawled about its sweating floor.

In the top room, under the ramshackle roof, lived an undergraduate (they are simply called students nowadays) named Napton. He had once gone with a University Expedition to North Africa, but had shacked up with a Tuareg woman for several months, and returned late for the start of the next University year, giving the excuse that his Land Rover had had a puncture. We all admired Napton. He was an original.

One day, when he was still in bed, the ceiling fell in on him.

Napton got up, dressed himself in one of the uniforms he collected, went out to his Land Rover which was parked in the Square, and drove off into the blue. He was away a year. I tried to salvage his things for him, and kept his collection of revolvers in my room. He presented me with a large brown teapot by way of thanks.

Below Napton lived an exotic of another hue, Nicholas Tanburn. He rarely left his room and subsisted solely on coffee. He was planning to go into oil in a big way after graduating. He lent me William Burroughs's *The Naked Lunch* which seemed a great deal of fun at the time.

But it was of Len Aitken and the other denizen of No. 12, Derick Grigs, that I saw most. We were united in drink and desperation. Griggy was a dear chap, beloved by all on the *Mail* and *Times*. He was making a small collection of

Japanese prints. Griggy remembered everything you said, and would quote it back to you, flatteringly, some years later. He was an amusing conversationalist, and any crisis would send him flying into a fit of calm. His sex life was a constant mystery to us. We had immense stamina at that time, staggering into bed in the early hours, rising zombie-like at eight. Len's room, by the look of it, had served as a set for a film of one of Gorki's or Dostoyevsky's more depressing ventures into the lower depths. Dozens of milk bottles full of cheese or urine stood on the bare boards. We got through life in the hope of more booze and each other's company. Not unlike the British Army, come to think of it.

Everyone on the *Mail* had good scripts in those days, and acted out striking character parts. I shared an office with two editors' secretaries, one of them Alison Britton, and her whippet. Whenever Alison was out of the room, Violet, the whippet, would leap across the top of the desks in a fit of mad gaiety. That dog really loved newspaper life. Alison decided to nip off to Rome with one of the reporters, and married him, although the marriage didn't hold up all that long, Anthony being more interested in cars. Anthony was notoriously vague, but the wedding celebrations were a wow, never to be forgotten. The reception was held out at Weston Manor, and we swam in champagne.

Anthony was the financial wizard. If his copy was half-an-hour late, it was early. Day after day, the Editor, Harford Thomas, would rave at Anthony. Then the copy would come through, brilliant as ever, and Harford and Anthony would sail off down the corridor, best of friends. Other chaps with staunch drinking habits included the poet, Adrian Mitchell, and D.A. Nicholas Jones, both of whom wrote novels while on the *Mail*.

When Anthony got a job in London, I raked a little bit of cash together, borrowed a bit more, and bought his house from him. It was one of a terrace of six, in Marston Street. There some of the crazier students founded the Oxford University Speculative Fiction Group, aided by C. S. Lewis and me. Lewis supplied the integrity, I supplied the booze.

Among our friends was the remarkable Kyril Bonfiglioli, then living in Norham Gardens with his second wife. Before his marriage he at one time lived in Jericho – a down-market sector of Oxford – with Anthony. They had Griggy as their lodger, though his habit of grilling kippers over the electric fire did not endear him to them. Dim indeed would be the man, and perhaps more especially the woman, who did not remember Bon forever after one meeting. It's a small world: Bon bought Sanders of Oxford, the bookshop where I had first worked, and set himself up as a bookseller.

Bon knew everything, particularly the everythings that no one else knew. His conversations ran on into the night, although this was often because they did not begin until 2:00 a.m., at which time he would turn up on your doorstep with a bottle of Glenfiddich, already broached. It was Bon who spotted a Giorgione, which he knew to be worth a half-million, lurking in a seedy Reading junk shop. The dealer wanted sixty pounds for it ('I believe as it was painted by a gentleman called Brown, sir, lived over Wallingford way, sir'). Bon knocked him down to forty.

Like J. G. Ballard, I got my early stories published in two magazines called *New Worlds* and *Science Fantasy*. These magazines were edited by Ted Carnell – the renowned E. J. Carnell. Carnell was good to his writers. I stayed with him when my marriage finally collapsed and my wife carted the children off to live at the seaside. Carnell was honest down to the last half-penny, and brought his magazines out regularly. He had no literary taste. When I submitted to him one of my best early short stories, 'The Failed Men', he wrote back saying, 'This will make you laugh. I hated your story and couldn't make sense of it but, since we were going to press and I was short by five thousand words, I shoved your effort in. Here's the cheque.' I didn't laugh. One wants appreciation as well as money. Particularly money on Carnell's miniscule scale.

The magazines slowly failed. Year by year, overheads mounted, sales slumped, Carnell himself became more locked into arthritis. He was always affable, with a good Cockney humour; everyone liked him. Eventually his parent firm sold the magazines. New editors were appointed by the new publisher. Much of this transaction took place in Oxford. It was arranged that Michael Moorcock, who had already made a name for himself, should edit *Science Fantasy*, and Bon *New Worlds*; however, owing to some misunderstanding, probably not unconnected with Glenfiddich, their roles were reversed. The magazines now went into new trajectories, *New Worlds* upwards, *Science Fantasy* downwards.

Meanwhile I was going to see my children as regularly as I could, and spending Christmas and other events like birthdays with them. Owing to the law of the land, this militated against divorce, since it implied that my wife and I were on amicable terms. She may not have been amicable, but she never drew the children into the quarrels. I was able to take Clive on trips to London and so on.

Wendy was growing bigger. She had been a baby when the axe fell; in despair, I had felt that it would be impossible to establish bonds of love with her. Also I realised how greatly my wife needed that small bundle of comfort. Wendy saw the situation differently. She was never in doubt that she loved and missed me. So she found her way to me. It was the first time in my life that love had come to me unearned and unpaid for.

Wendy grew to look remarkably like my sister Betty. Betty, meanwhile, was working in London. My mother had sensibly rented out her house in Oxford and was living the life of Riley in a flat in Hammersmith, popping into pubs for lunch, chatting to all and sundry, and taking trips abroad – notably Italy, which she loved, since the waiters were more friendly than in England. And it was a bit sunnier, of course.

The agony of having to be separated from my children never quite left me – and can still blaze up even now as I think of it – but somehow times improved. One omen of the happiness to come was the appearance of a female kitten I called Nicky, who arrived unbidden one evening at my house in Marston Street. She was a special and mysterious cat who lived with me for some thirteen years, and became to some extent an embodiment, an anima, of a new woman in my life, Margaret.

The sixties came in like a spring tide. Poor worried depressed England – for a few years at least – became an exciting and positive place in which to live. Harold Wilson's two terms as Prime Minister have since been marked down as a time of fraudulent economic practices. That may have been; I am no judge. But a longer view may perceive that oddly classless man as exactly suited to preside over a time when, for many people, the bounds of life extended, horizons opened, new life-styles became possible. The Beatles' music, too, was classless, and a suitable accompaniment to a fresh way of looking at things.

In the other arts, too, there was what George Melly called

a 'revolt into style'. We found a new way of interpreting science fiction to go with the times. In *Greybeard*, I developed the means of exorcising my loss of children by universalising that experience; but even as I was shaping the last adjective, I had in mind a newer sleeker model, which emerged as *The Dark Light Years*. Both novels were published in 1964. A growing reputation encouraged one to do great mad things. Novels were easy to write in those days; they become more difficult as one's thought becomes more complex.

After many struggles and several jobs, my sister Betty – whose dress sense was all mine was not – got a job with BBC-TV as a costume designer. There she did brilliant work over the years, notably the designs for a very successful series, *The Duchess of Duke Street*. Her favourite period was Victorian, although she did Restoration plays (Sheridan's *The Critic*, for instance), and some modern stuff, including working with the marvellous Ronnie Barker on *Porridge*, his prison comedy series. As my marriage broke up after the death of my father, so Betty married only when my mother died, in the late seventies. She had plenty of boyfriends. In her Oxford days, there was a good supply. In 1952 she was going about with the handsome and distinguished Zulfikar Ali Bhutto, later to be President of Pakistan. On one occasion when father was still alive, she brought Bhutto home for a sherry, since father's hospitality did not run to much else. It could be said of my father by way of criticism that he was not much of a Glenfiddich man. After Betty and Bhutto had left for some glossier night-spot, father said, 'What next? Now she's bringing the wogs home . . .' Well, some attitudes have improved since then. Even sectarian violence has become unacceptable.

Bonfiglioli somewhat neglected his editing and possibly

his bookselling. He had hit upon – with Bon one uses the verb instinctively – an absolutely irresistible lady, the veritable dark lady of the sonnets herself. Occasionally there are girls off whom it is impossible to keep one's hands; reason does not supply an answer to this fascinating conundrum. Probably the imponderable pressure of the pheromones has much to do with it. So many of my best friends are shits; I have decided that pheromones are the answer to why we choose here, reject there. Pheromones are probably responsible for all human history.

Anyhow, I had also met my irresistible girl, a Scots lass called Margaret. Helen Shapiro, aged sixteen, was singing about 'Walking Back to Happiness', unaware that the Beatles were about to doom her to tour Australia for ever. I took the song, innocent that I was, as an omen that I should allow myself to be happy with Margaret and cease the grieving for my children. I was very unforgiving with myself. Many years later, going to do a broadcast in London, I went into a studio and found them playing 'Walking Back to Happiness'. There was Helen Shapiro, still young and attractive. When I told her of my passionate fandom, she fell into my arms in gratitude. I gave her a copy of *Helliconia Spring* on the spot, but she never wrote.

With Margaret, life went on to the same sort of trajectory as *New Worlds*. Upwards. England appeared to be going the same way. Harold Wilson was Prime Minister. Harold took me in, hook, line and sinker. I actually believed in the white heat of Britain's technological revolution. I really liked Harold and his buddy George Brown. The latter I met later in the House of Lords, a bit ripe on the old Glenfiddich. He wasn't as pretty as Helen Shapiro, but just as much fun in his way.

Something had to be done about the stalemate in my life, otherwise Margaret was not going to wait. She had been secretary to Lord Harewood, and John Tooley at Covent Garden Opera House, and obviously had higher expectations than I ever did. But those dread words had been spoken to me: 'If I can't have you, I'll see to it that no other woman ever does.' Perhaps they were delivered first in some Victorian melodrama. I once saw Tod Slaughter, towards the end of his career, performing his star role in *Sweeney Todd*; he had lines of the kind to utter. But the words still held a chill in the early sixties, when the divorce laws gave them bite.

Flitting abroad seemed a good idea. The epoch was dawning when people did funny things to themselves with flowers, beads, dope and hair. Time to be off.

So I learnt to drive, bought a secondhand Land Rover, and took Margaret away – to Jugoslavia for six months. We did it all on about £120. Most of the time we camped, sometimes we stayed in a hotel to get a shower.

Jugoslavia in 1964 was still pulling itself out of the festival of destruction which it had experienced in the war years. Many of its cities, from Maribor in the north to Prilep in the south, presented images of decrepitude. New building was austere. Roads and factories were built by amateur youth or army groups. Communism was still doctrinaire; portraits of Tito were everywhere. We arrived in March in a snowstorm.

It is impossible to lose the past, one's individual past or the past of a country. The Balkans possess great natural beauty combined with a history of bloodshed. Six republics comprise modern Jugoslavia – Slovenia, Croatia, Serbia, Montenegro, Macedonia, and Bosnia. Each republic has a different history. This difference is often expressed in most radical terms, in religion, in language. Margaret and I found that traces of the Byzantine past still lingered, and the days of the medieval Serbian state, when the Nemanija dynasty ruled. I wrote a short story on this theme, 'The Day of the Doomed King'.

All the republics have their attractions. Bosnia, though Communist, is also Muslim, so it is hard to get a drink there; the highlands are austerely beautiful. We long to go back to its remoter regions. Montenegro, or Crna Gora, means the Black Mountain, a fitting description. Macedonia is lovely and wild; when we were there, the beautiful bagrems (acacias) flowered, exuding a heavier scent than they can manage in an English lane. The coast of Dalmatia is world-famous.

Our vehicle had painted on its doors OXFORD–OHRID in Roman and Cyrillic script. Ohrid, on Lake Ohrid, was our furthest point. You stand on the shore of this miniature Mediterranean and look across the water to the unforgiving mountains of Albania, which clothe their peaks in snow even in mid-summer. Many years later, Wendy and her husband Mark have also made it to Ohrid. It is still an inaccessible and gentle spot. In Ohrid, the tasty lake trout were once caught, to be wrapped in moist leaves and carried alive by runners to the courts of Constantinople.

We lived a rather gipsy life, a bit like Burma sans bullets, often camping in the middle of nowhere or, even worse, on the perimeters of nowhere. Or we would camp in the grounds of a monastery, or by the Adriatic, rising for an early morning swim. We lived on the harsh bread of the country, with a chunk of salami, a bottle of rich local wine and maybe some chocolate (Kras orange chocolate from Zagreb preferred).

Plus plenty of slivovic to keep the germs away. It was the diet of many Jugoslavs. We kept very fit on it, though we lost a lot of weight.

On the way home, at the port of Makarska, under the austere putty walls of the karst, Margaret and I met up with Harry and Joan Harrison. They were living in Denmark. Since we had no address, there was no chance of two-way communication, but we had dropped them a line to Rungsted Kyst, asking them to meet us at twelve noon in Makarska camp site (the existence of which we hypothesized) on a certain day in July. We found the camp, rolled into it, and within five minutes the Harrisons also arrived in their Volkswagen camper. There was reason to celebrate.

Harry has somehow eluded me in this account so far. In life, it was different. We first met at a World Science Fiction Convention in London in 1957, and have been friends ever since. Harry had newly discovered the world; he had received a cheque from John W. Campbell on *Astounding* for his story 'The Stainless Steel Rat'. and had plonked the money down for a one-way ticket to Europe. Harry and I felt contempt for most sf authors, who buzz about the galaxy on paper, yet are afraid to venture into the world in real life. Harry went everywhere, spoke all languages, including Esperanto. Harry is the life force incarnate. He taught me how to enjoy life.

It was Harry who had first driven me into Jugoslavia, with Kingsley Amis and the girls, in 1963. There on a remote Croatian hillside, with the cicadas serenading somnolence, we had our taste of the south. It wasn't quite the Far East, but at least it had once been known as the Near East.

William Kinglake's wonderful book *Eothen* opens with him leaving wheel-borne Europe and crossing the Danube to the plague-bound fortress of Belgrade, then only recently liberated from Turkish rule. For the mid-century Victorians, the Near East began in what is now Jugoslavia. One can still see what they meant, though the minarets start a little farther south, in Prijedor and Sarajevo.

Kinglake was one reason, apart from Harry, why we went to Jugoslavia. With Harry and Joan we sailed over to the beautiful Adriatic islands of Cres and Losinj, where ladies from the Viennese court had once spent their languid Dual Monarchic summers. When we were there, the crowds on the quaysides were singing Chubby Checker numbers. The great ironing out of the world was in process.

Back in England towards the end of 1964 we found that the first issue of Mike Moorcock's *New Worlds* was published. I settled in to write up my travel notes, to turn them into the book called *Cities and Stones* which Faber published in 1965, illustrated by Margaret's and my photographs. We planned other travel books. Turkey was on our list. And Brazil. But it didn't quite work out that way.

The Jug trip left us with an abiding love of Jugoslavia, which remained even after my book was banned in Belgrade. Now all is forgiven, and a new generation regards my book as a truthful and, I hope, generous account of what their country was like at that time. Which is pleasing, for I owe a great deal to that trip and what it taught me about the running of a country, of history and geography, and of a great many other things. Hardly a novel written since has not contained something of Jugland, as we affectionately call it. For instance the story of King Jandal Anganol's child marriage in *Helliconia Summer* is based rather remotely on the story of King Milutin long ago in the medieval Serbian state.

*   *   *

With science fiction, there has always been a cause, a battle. It is not considered 'respectable' reading. Yet the subject matter of good science fiction is the subject matter of our time. Science fiction readers, banding together as fans, formed a strong support group for their writers, editors and publishers; many of them grew to fill those vital roles themselves. Science fiction fandom encompasses the most active and concerned readership one can meet. They collect, they catalogue, they throw tremendous parties and conventions. Lucky sf writers, to receive such support.

Lucky sf writers, too, to be invited abroad to meet foreign fans. One of the best such shindigs ever thrown was in Rio de Janeiro in 1969. The cast of thousands included Robert Heinlein, Poul Anderson, John Brunner, Damon Knight, A. E. van Vogt, and Robert Sheckley. Harry was also there, and Ballard and I flew in together from England. Was it there I met Frederik Pohl for the first time? We became friends, decided we liked the jet-set life, and determined to meet somewhere else the following year.

Working at long distance, we persuaded a Japanese fan, Hiroya Endo, to start an sf symposium in Japan to coincide with Expo 70. Endo worked the Miracle. With Sakyo Kumatsu as chairman, we duly met. Fred took his wife Carol with him. Judith Merril, one of the great propagandists for Moorcock's New Wave, was also there, and Arthur C. Clarke. There we met some of our Russian equivalents, the doleful Dr Eremi Parnov, the genial and learned Julius Kagarlitski, whom I already knew and greatly liked, and the forceful Vasili Zakharchenko, then a TV personality and editor of a popular science journal which sold two million copies every month. A great deal of international toasting went on.

We visited Tokyo, Toyota Motor City, and Kyoto, where

we were taken to the extraordinary Expo 70. The futuristic parts of the Mitsubishi tower were designed by Komatsu. Even more impressive, we met our Japanese publishers, who had put out our work magnificently, in leather-bound editions. Well, mock-leather.

On the way home from Japan, I stopped for a week in Hong Kong, to visit friends, the Toogoods, and see how Hong Kong had fared since I knew it at the end of the war, when the Japanese had reduced it to a vast rubbish pile.

Sitting next to me on the plane from Tokyo was a small Indian lady, very ascetic in appearance, her grey hair scraped back into a bun, dressed in a plain sari, and wearing steel-rimmed spectacles on her sharp nose. We talked casually at first, and then intensely. She had been to the shrines of Kyoto, to reinforce her faith.

She spoke simply; wit – an unexpected way of putting ordinary things – salted her conversation. It was rather like talking to Gandhi. I was conscious of the greedy indulgence of the West, of which I was representative. This lady was sketching a more elegant style, with much that I admired: many cultural activities, self-abnegation, formal relationships within a large family, occasional festivals. She lived with her sisters and other relations, her husband being dead, some distance outside Bombay.

'Why do you not come to stay with me for a while?' she asked me. 'You can easily send a telegram to your wife, explaining.'

But what would the cable have said? A door had opened for me. I remembered H. G. Wells's short story, 'The Door in the Wall'. The plane was descending, preparing to land at Kai Tak.

'I have friends awaiting me in Hong Kong,' I said.

The door closed.

Since then, I have seen the door again. Never have I ventured through it. Never has there been enough time. Every year is busier than the last. It has been my fortune, through the success of my writing, to travel to many parts of the world.

In 1979 I visited China, more or less under the aegis of the late Felix Greene. Felix was a saint, though many people thought him a deluded one. He had the difficult role of being 'Friend of China'. His position was, Your country right or wrong. By espousing China, Felix also espoused some of the larger madnesses of Mao Zedong. Judgement is a fine quality, but does not rank as high as devotion. Those of us who saw China through his eyes loved him. He died in 1985 of cancer in Mexico, with his wife Elena to look after him.

China puts its mark on everyone. Everything is seen anew. An old fence is not an old fence but a fence that has weathered many Chinese years. Everything is different – yet not alien, as may be the case in Japan. The sounds, the light, the smells . . . well, they have their quality which is not easily conveyed, just as some wines do not travel.

Among our small party were Iris Murdoch, Michael Young – now Lord Young of Dartington – David Attenborough – now knighted – and Maysie Webb, deputy Director of the British Museum. We were granted audience with Chairman Deng Xao-Ping. At that time, China was a great novelty place, on everyone's lips, and we were unduly favoured. Awaiting audience with the great man was much like awaiting audience with one of the Ming emperors. We kicked our heels and speculated and grumbled and sent messages, just as did travellers in earlier centuries. I made a side trip on my own to Shanghai to see American friends, Philip and Sue Smith, who were teaching English to the Chinese students via science fiction. My present for them was twenty-four copies of my *Penguin Science Fiction Omnibus*, which has been in print for over a quarter of a century.

Life was very hard for the Chinese people. 'Eat bitterness,' is what children are taught. We found they liked the English sense of humour. The Smiths' students were so poor they often sat in the evening to drink 'white tea', as they called it – hot water to which no tea leaf has been added. Their attitudes to sex were very strait-laced. Whether this was provoked in part by the crowded conditions in the cities, one cannot determine. Change is taking place rapidly. All the same, no one can imagine a China that is no longer China. It is a most wonderful country. One gives one's heart to it and its people. Our group all wept when we had to say goodbye to Mr Wang, our civilised and witty guide, at Guanzou railway station.

China has held a fascination for me since an early age. Nor was it a disappointment. I might say much the same about the United States. Most of the lively arts I enjoyed as a child came from the U.S.A.: the films, popular music, jazz, comic strips like Bill Holman's 'Smokey Stover', and, of course, science fiction magazines. Margaret and I visited the States first in 1965, to collect a Nebula Award for my novella, *The Saliva Tree*. Since then I return regularly, and have many friends there, though there was a time when almost no one in sf wanted to know me. It means something to have a reputation there as well as in my own country. The three books published on my writing have all appeared only in the States – though the most comprehensive one, *Apertures*, is by my English friend, David Wingrove.

My travels took me to Australia and I even went back to Sumatra to revisit old haunts and discover new ones – especially the amazing Lake Toba in the Highlands. That is a story in itself.

Wherever I have been, without exception, I have observed two things: the beauty of the smallest manifestations of nature, and the difficulty or downright wretchedness which still attends the lives of most people – though the 'quiet desperation' which Thoreau observed in men's lives appears to be endured with more fortitude in the East than in the West.

Harry, Fred Pohl and I, together with Peter Kuczka of Hungary and some others, got together to found World SF. Harry was its first president, then Fred, then I; now it is Sam Lundwall of Sweden. The objective of World SF is to link anyone in the world who has an interest in sf literature which transcends national boundaries. It is open to professionals only. Politics add to the difficulties in this sphere as in many others, but still we are a great success and have met in several different countries in our short existence, to communicate and bestow awards.

There are advantages in having one's books translated into many languages, and to find that those same books are reprinted at home over and over again. Some of my short story collections have been in print for twenty-five years. Even my 'difficult' novels like *Report on Probability A* are continuously reprinted – to my surprise, for many of my books had to be fought for on their first appearance.

My relationship with fandom was not always smooth. Given the freedom to write, one must be wild and free. Carnell's reception of 'The Failed Men' in no way discouraged me. I wrote whole novels he could not abide. And by then he had become my literary agent. He thought *Dark Light Years* disgusting and *Report on Probability A* incomprehensible. The latter was turned down by Faber, though they published it six years later, after Mike printed it in *New Worlds*. *Probability A* marked my commitment to bringing art and artistic concerns into sf. But fans heartily disliked the book. When *Probability A* was followed a little later by the Acid Head War stories, also in *New Worlds*, and when they appeared in novel form as *Barefoot in the Head*, fury broke out, and I was practically drummed out of the regiment. Fresh fury when my history of sf, *Billion Year Spree*, appeared; evidently I had not toed the party line. My history is civilised, intelligent, and entertaining. The comments I received were not.

The rule in life is to soldier on. The Forgotten Army taught you that. Margaret and I got married at last, and her parents gave us a great splurge at the Randolph Hotel in Oxford. Margaret's parents were Scots, and very generous to us. We had to leave the hotel at three-thirty to catch a plane to Paris, where we were honeymooning. As we left, the champagne corks were still popping. It is one of the cheeriest sounds in the world.

The difficulties of past years were behind me. I was forty. I had my marvellous Margaret. Among her other qualities, she immediately accepted Clive and Wendy and always loved it when they came to stay. We took them abroad and had many happy times. Writing at that period had not devoured my life. It was the time of the Harold Wilson government. For us, England was a sunny place. Hilary Rubinstein, Victor Gollancz's nephew, bought a partnership in the oldest literary agency, A. P. Watt, and I joined him. Hilary is the best of agents and friends. Feeling that it was increasingly impossible to write sf, I turned to ordinary fiction and, over the seventies, wrote three novels about Horatio Stubbs, whose career markedly parallels mine in some respects. They were *The Hand-Reared Boy*, *A Soldier Erect*, and *A Rude Awakening*. The first two topped the best-seller list, and I enjoyed my fame. The third got nowhere. It was my Sumatra novel. At last I had written it, thirty years after leaving those steamy shores; perhaps the communiqué arrived a little too late.

Margaret and I have lived in several houses. We enjoy the change of ambience. Jasmine House was a lovely thatched Tudor cottage, near Oxford but seemingly isolated. We have always resisted the lure of living in London, or the equally strong attraction of escaping swingeing British taxes by living abroad.

After Jasmine came our favourite house, Heath House at Southmoor, a darling place where all the top floor was my study. We were away from other houses and could have huge noisy summer parties outside in the courtyard. There were lots of friends around, some good, some bad. We were quite trendy; at one time, tiring of our first names, we attempted to persuade people to use our middle names, Chris and Wilson. Only my old friend Anthony Price, now also a successful writer, obliged for long.

With my mother failing in health and the kids needing good schools, we moved into Oxford. Oh, yes, the kids! First Timothy, at whose birth I was present through what was a long ordeal for Margaret. Clive was glad that it was a boy; Wendy said, 'Please make the next one a girl for me.' Margaret obliged – to such an extent that Charlotte was born on the morning of Wendy's tenth birthday. Charlotte has her sister's sanguine temperament. When watching the

TV weather chart with a promise of snow about, she cried (age six): 'Goodee – sleet!'

My mother fell ill when I was at a conference in Sicily. Fortunately Margaret was around. I returned on the Monday to find mother barely conscious; but the doctor was so optimistic that I was scarcely more than concerned. At the time, I was Chairman of the Committee of Management of the Society of Authors; next day, the Tuesday, I had to attend an AGM to deliver the annual report. Margaret said, as I went to the car, 'You must go and see your mother before you head for London. You never know what may happen.'

I have always been grateful for that advice. I picked a red rose for my mother, peeled off the thorns and went round to the home where she lay. She could just acknowledge my presence. Somewhere, wherever she was, she knew I was there. I pressed the rose into her plump little hand and soon had to rush for the London train. That afternoon, just as I was preparing to get on the platform with the AGM report, one of the Society women told me (against Margaret's instructions) that Margaret had phoned through to say my mother had died. It was a good moment to practise soldiering on.

By mother's bedside lay the last book I had bought her. She wanted a Dickens. I chose *Hard Times*, which she had not read. I regretted that I had not made a more cheerful choice. Inside the copy were sheets of paper with the last word games she had been playing to keep herself amused. I still have them.

Something of this event and this time I wrote into my non-sf novel, *Life in the West*. That book did well in Britain, and was chosen by Anthony Burgess as one of his '99 Best Novels since 1939'. It's a shame it was never published in the States, since it is very much a novel of thought and feeling. Perhaps the way I have been type-cast as a mere sf writer did not help my cause.

We moved outside Oxford again, to a lovely stone house, three centuries old, near Woodstock. In its garden was a marvellous heated swimming pool, our delight. Timothy and Charlotte spent a whole summer in the water. But disaster struck us at Orchard House. We had accrued massive tax debts, through the inefficiency of our accountants, which suddenly became due. The British economy was going down the drain yet again. There was no money. My name in the States, where it had once stood higher than in England, was down to zero. We had to sell up and move back to a smaller house in North Oxford.

So it goes, as Vonnegut used to say. At least we were near to my Aunt Dorothy, who had shared her house with my mother. We could keep an eye on her. By hard and constant work, we dug ourselves out of the hole we were in. Margaret works with me in the study, and is the super-woman version of a word-processor. At present she is also compiling my bibliography. Although I seem to have written a great deal, some of our happiest times have been while there is a novel 'up the go' as they put it. There is always pleasure in coming down in the morning to a new sheet of paper, new possibilities, new opportunities to surprise the world and oneself.

Margaret's mother still lives in Oxford. Otherwise the old generation has gone. We have to face it that, in the eyes of all but ourselves, we are the older generation. We're in the firing line. Clive is teaching English in Athens, Wendy has recently married Mark and returned from a tour of the Far East, photographing all the way. This very night, we shall see the films she shot in China. She too has been to Burma.

Timothy and Charlotte are at school. We have survived terrible teenage parties. Soon, they will be going into the world. All four of my dearly loved children get on well together, and will help one another in times of trouble. Split-level families were once unusual. Now they seem to be the norm, and the old nuclear family as depicted so winningly, so hygienically, on the back of cornflake packets is no more. People have better chances than they did to work through their mistakes and rectify them if possible. The slackening of conformity has been a fructifying thing.

In the summer of 1984, when *Helliconia* was finished, we sold our North Oxford house and bought another mansion we could not, by any realistic accountancy, afford. But it was love at first sight with Woodlands. We are back outside Oxford, with trees round about and a copse at the bottom of the garden. There's space to breathe; architects and craftsmen cared about the building of the house back in 1907, before the First World War, when the world changed. We shall not always need such a large house, but at present we have the excuse.

My tortured interior life of long ago is remembered only when I sketch in a reconstruction here. I even got rid of God, that old spectre from East Dereham, this year. He has haunted my novels as he has me. But in *Helliconia* I worked my way through to what I really believe.

Much of that new-found belief is grounded in a complex response to nature, and the workings of the planet. The scientist Jim Lovelock, in his book *Gaia*, expresses beautifully the way in which living species form part of a self-regulating system which keeps Earth's biosphere habitable for its tremendous diversity of life. We all, before we are born, have to work our way up to consciousness from molecular levels of being. After life, we shall sink back to them again.

Standing among the trees in our copse as dark comes on, I sense with my entire being the presence of Gaia. We are in kinship – in league with – all else that lives in nature, including the invisible microscopic life which in total far outweighs all visible living things. We are not eternal. Seventy years and we are spent: consciousness is too delicate a balancing act to endure. But we are composed of things that are eternal. Part of us has never died.

For more of this kind of mysticism, you must consult the three volumes of *Helliconia* where the argument is better, because less briefly, deployed. To worry about death is useless. But by worrying about life, we can shape ourselves, at least for a while, into what we want and need to be.

The *New York Times* book critic, Gerald Jonas, concluded a full page of praise for *Helliconia* with the words, 'I would say that Mr Aldiss is now in competition with no one but himself.' Welcome praise. But aren't writers always in competition only with themselves?

What do my books, what does my life amount to? I always wished to be someone. I felt myself less than the dust. My wish was to help, to reach out generously, to give generously. As I was impatient with East Dereham and the narrowness of its mores, later I became impatient with England. The impatience extends to my writing. Why is it not better, harsher?

Jules Verne ran away to sea, but was taken home by his father before the vessel sailed. He wrote novels of travel for the rest of his life.

It cannot be said that my fiction does not take large subjects. The truths it tells are generally symbolic ones. It is not literal, though it uses an abbreviated realism to convey its inferences. Its closeness – or its distance – from the events which inspired it is unimportant. It forms a kind of substitute reality, a gloss on real experience. It seeks to crystallise.

Perhaps for readers it works this way. It does for me. Only after I had completed *A Rude Awakening* was I able to return to Sumatra. Only after I had worked for many years on *Helliconia* was I able to walk on the ground which inspired the name, Mount Helicon, in Greece.

And for a writer, his writing has also a more direct, less mystical function.

My wish was always somehow to restore the scattered family – an impossible ambition. I am a rare writer. For many years, I have written what I chose, defying editors and fate, a poor man's intellectual, famous but only slightly famous, with nothing of my work filmed or televised. If no great sums of money have come my way, I have kept my family from starving.

Now I read about the Shelley circle. Margaret and I exchange Mary Shelley's collected letters, a life of Claire Clairmont, essays, Shelley's poems, Byron's letters. An intensely creative group of personalities, too soon destroyed by fate. Yet their interest lives on. That is something to leave behind.

In concluding this sketch, I cannot but note that there is much pain in it. So there is in any truthful autobiographical account. For many years, I was unable to deal with the pain I experienced, and unable to communicate it. Like

Frankenstein's monster, I felt malicious because I was miserable – the very reverse of Christian doctrine. And my difficulty was the monster's: parental coldness.

On these difficulties I had to build my life. Being only too aware that I have survived in an age when so many millions of lives have been shattered by war, I must not emphasise either my difficulties or my successes. Exile means a loss of home. But I built my home in writing, and achieved security there, both for myself and my family, in 'the Republic of Letters and the Kingdom of Dreams'.

As to the durable qualities of those writings – they were built to last in these transitory times. Whether they will do so is not up to me to judge, but to the Twenty-First Century.

Acknowledgements

The origins of these articles are as follows:

'Bold Towers, Shadowed Streets' © 1986 Brian W. Aldiss.

'. . . And the Lurid Glare of the Comet' © 1986 Brian W. Aldiss. Previously as Introduction to H.G. Wells: *In the Days of the Comet*, Chatto & Windus, London, 1985.

'When the Future Had to Stop' © 1986 Brian W. Aldiss. Previously as a review in *Vogue*.

'What Happens Next?' © 1986 Brian W. Aldiss. Previously as a speech delivered in 1980.

'Grounded in Stellar Art' © 1986 Brian W. Aldiss.

'It Takes Time to Tango' © 1986 Brian W. Aldiss. Previously in *The Guardian*.